POLES APART
ON THE SAME BED

Twenty-Nine Selected Short Stories

by
Alexander Raju

Selected and Introduced by
S. Subhash Chandran

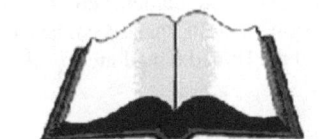

CCB Publishing
British Columbia, Canada

Poles Apart on the Same Bed: Twenty-Nine Selected Short Stories

Copyright ©2011 by Alexander Raju
ISBN-13   978-1-926918-66-2
First Edition

Library and Archives Canada Cataloguing in Publication
Raju, Alexander, 1952-
Poles apart on the same bed : twenty-nine selected short stories /
by Alexander Raju; selected and introduced by S. Subhash Chandran.
ISBN 978-1-926918-66-2
I. Chandran, S. Subhash II. Title.
PR9499.4.R35P64 2011   823'.92   C2011-905639-9

Cover image, *Melancholy* by Italian Baroque artist Domenico Fetti (c. 1589-1623), is in the public domain.

Publisher: CCB Publishing
               British Columbia, Canada
               www.ccbpublishing.com

Dedicated to all my dear and near ones - my parents and siblings, my wife and children, my friends and relatives, my teachers and former colleagues and thousands of my former students.

Other works by Alexander Raju

The Haunted Man (1997, 2009)

Upon This Bank and Shoal (2008)

When Babel Tower Is Falling Down

And Still Plays the Abyssinian Damsel on Her Dulcimer

Ripples and Pebbles (1989)

The Sprouts of Indignation (2003)

The Magic Chasm (2007)

The Psycho-Social Interface in British Fiction (2000)

The Voice of Ethiopia (ed. 2008)

PREFACE

Alexander Raju's *Poles Apart on the Same Bed* is a finely made selection of his stories written over thirty years—ranging between the stories of a tyro giving expression to his idealistic perspective of the world and the society he lives in and intensely feels about, and those of a cynical angry man in quarrel with the world and its ways. They are poles apart also in the sense that the stories do not belong to any particular school: they range from humorous musings on the stupidity of men and women of his social milieu to harsh diatribes against the many evils rampant in his society. There are stories with what the author calls "gothic elements"—stories with an eerie air of horror in them. There are overtones of his Christian upbringing in the sense that he makes recurrent allusions to biblical parables. At the same time, he frequently deals with essentially Indian (Hindu) myths/beliefs/superstitions. The title story (number 22) deals literally with the condition of a representative couple living together, having slept on and shared the same bed; but the pondering hero realizes they have been poles apart all their lives when you look at it beneath the make-belief marital calm. Some stories are sheer fantasy: beyond our normal reasoning. These stories falling under different heads have one binding chord: they relate to the social realities of Kerala, the south Indian state.

The most emotionally appealing are the author's renditions of the plight of the helpless female, sexually exploited by the male-dominated society. Many stories belong to this group. They are particularly poignant since they fictionalize not any feminist idea, but everyday reality we witness in our quotidian existence. "The Sobbing Guitar", for example, cannot be read without being shocked: the suicide of a young Anglo-Indian girl ditched by her lover. "Through the Fog" tells the story of an old father and his prostitute daughter who sells her body to earn their daily bread. "The Roof Frame" is the story of a carpenter's grief whose daughter finds solace in suicide since she is made pregnant by the master's son. Lying on his death bed he is remembering omens that were always there of an impending tragedy, which he failed to associate with his own young daughter. "The Icy Decision" is the story of a father and daughter who commit suicide together, again following the helplessness of the daughter being blackmailed by a lover-turned-rogue. The most poignant of this category of stories are "Before the Cock Crew Twice" and "A Call from the Black Crows." Both these stories tell the violent deaths suffered by two daughters who eloped with cheats and were deserted. All these stories are told from the point of view of the agonized father reliving the pity and horror in his memories.

Yet another concern voiced by the author in more than one story is the plight of the destitute in contemporary society. "The Star Night" and "The Vendor of Tooth Powder" are stories of this category that bewail the destitution and starvation of the underprivileged in our society. At times, the author looks at ordinary things and events in a light-hearted vein and verbalizes his views more with bemused contempt than censor. "Fate of People in the Land of Coconut Trees" and "A Simple Cure for Pimples" are hilarious narratives of this sort. The author is critical of objectionable practices and attitudes and he puts them before us without any moralizing about them. "The Last Temptation of Joseph Rich" exposes the unquenchable greed and avarice of the modern man. "Liquor Tragedy or the Direction of a Murder" is a mixture of humor and horror in that the author humorously draws our attention to the dangers of alcohol consumption.

"A Jasmine on the Basil Plant Pedestal" is written in

revolutionary fervor that calls for an end to the apartheid in the caste-ridden Hindu society.

There are a few stories that the author likes to describe as having a gothic element in them. These stories begin in the normal narrative tone, but at some stage after halfway, they strain all our logic and turn eerily horrible. "The Verdict and a Few Hailstones" thus ends when the protagonist—a woman—melts into thin air in the presence of the author/narrator. "The Story of a Sale" leaves you horror-stricken when the narrator tells you that a butcher drags the narrator's wife to the slaughter house instead of a goat he had sold. "The End of an Evangelist" also ends when the narrator finds his wife and child being put to fire. "The Junction" is a revenge story with all the horror elements. The collection ends significantly with a story that takes the reader to the world after death. It is sheer fantasy mixed with a wry humor. The narrator who expected peace in Heaven finds himself being surrounded by his kith and kin and a nagging wife. He seems to ask, *what is this heaven for?*

This collection of stories is sure to offer some good reading to readers of all tastes. I wish this venture of Alexander Raju all success.

S. Subhash Chandran

CONTENTS

PART ONE

Selected from Stories Written

Between 1981 and 2000

1

THE VERDICT AND A FEW HAILSTONES

After passing the verdict, the court adjourned for lunch. A shocking silence prevailed in the air.

The members of the public who rushed to the court premises and elbowed at the windows to watch the agony of the defendant as well as the helplessness of the defendant's advocate became thoroughly disappointed. They stood here and there in small groups, engaged in heated discussions and zealous whisperings on the incompetence of the judge, the incapability of the public prosecutor, the indifference of the police and the cunningness of the defendant's lawyer.

Holding tightly together the seams of my loose black gown, I stared at the face of my client. It took minutes for me to believe that it was my robe that had saved her from the hangman's noose.

But she, without any delicacy, came out of the defendant's box like a mad woman, seized my hand and then pulled and dragged me through the angry mob towards the parking area in front of the court.

Being speechless in utter amazement, I walked behind her in quick strides, cursing the palm of my right hand which was crushed under her strong grip. As I was moving, my eyes were fixed at the darkness of her disheveled curly hair and I felt as if I were becoming smaller and smaller and, at last, like a child trailing behind his mother holding the edge of her sari. I lisped and whined over something or other and turned my head towards the dark clouds thickening in the sky.

I felt that she was quite indifferent to my resistance. Opening the car door, she pushed me into the front seat and, later, sprang into the driver's seat. It was only then that I noticed the exact expression on her face. Her crazy eyes were looking for the head of the road that was destined to be crushed under the wheels of the car. When she smiled like those who had forgotten to smile, and thereby, distorted her face, I was wondering what might be the measurement of her braziers! What else should I have to do?

Realizing that the car which was dashing and roaring like a drunkard would, perhaps, darken the future of hers, mine and of a few pedestrians, I moved towards her and sat closer. I noticed that she was swaying and shaking her head like a hysterical woman. I was frightened seeing the steering wheel that slipped at times from her hands.

She laughed aloud and began talking: "Now, why should you be afraid, my dear lawyer? Er....! Well! Let it be there! Hmm....! I think you have completely forgotten my case! The honorable court agreed when you and I said that the pistol presented in the court was a mere toy-pistol, didn't they? Well....! In fact, my dear advocate, did you too believe that?"

Having no courage to look at her face, I sat motionless, watching in the direction of the car, counting the lamp-posts that swiftly passed by and absorbing heat from the fleshy folds of her waist through my right elbow!

With a frightening laugh, she continued: "Take that toy-pistol with both your hands, raise it up to your face, meditate for a moment and, then, say, 'Open Sesame'. Then you can see how the real pistol emerges out of its broken frame.....! Ha! Ha...!"

A moment passed and a serene expression came on her face. I gawked at her rosy lips; they were trembling as if whispering some chants. I strained my ears to hear what she was saying in a hissing voice: "It's just simple as this! Your study cell must be silent! Sit by the desk where you shove your books! Seize the secret skull from the chest of drawers, scour it with your hands and stare at its mesmeric shape! Concentrate for a second and say, 'Open Sesame'. Then you see how life comes to that erstwhile useless skull! So simple, isn't it?"

I was shocked. I pressed the car's brake, placing my right foot over her left foot. Our car screeched to a stop, brushing lightly against a band of coolies who were standing in the middle of the road, talking and arguing, perhaps, over their labor problems.

The frightened laborers stood stupefied and wonderstruck for a moment. Then, as they were furiously hitting and kicking on our car, as an outlet for their emotions on chance-escaping, and were showering vituperations on us in their strange vernacular, a cold wind began to blow from somewhere, howling like a werewolf.

The cold wind swept across the street and then disappeared. Soon a mist began to spread and cover the street. Suddenly, she got out onto the road as if to say something to the disturbed coolies, leaving me alone in the car. As the asphalted main road steamed in the drizzle, the laborers ran towards the verandah of the nearby shops in order to save their heads from the hailstones that seemed to be thrown down by someone through the mist. She alone stood in that deserted street, with hands raised up to the sky, like a Greek marble statue.

I felt that she was laughing aloud and whispering something inaudibly. I noticed her eyes losing their brightness and, in the thickness of the mist, her body turning gray and dark.

The hailstones drummed a pit-pat rhythm on the top of the car. In the cold storm, her white clothes fluttered and loosened and separated, and then, dissolved into the intensity of the grey mist. Her naked body, gradually disintegrated, the flesh falling down from the bones and the bones slipping away from their joints, and melting and vanishing like the hailstones that lay on the road. Only the waves of her laughter that reverberated in the street together with the storm's howling echoed inside the car for a moment. Then, they too entered through my ears and became etched in the memory of my brain.

Author's notes: In India, we have Right-Hand Drive. I love to read this story backward, from the last sentence to the first one!

2

THE LAST TEMPTATION OF JOSEPH RICH

During the small hours of that Easter Sunday, when the holy rites and ceremonies at the church came to an end, Joseph Rich walked hurriedly towards his bank. As a busy banker who gave money to the needy by accepting gold ornaments in lien, how many account books had he to deal with! And for a true businessman, was there any rest in life?

Was it not his hard work for day and night as well as his unmistakable calculations that helped him to own a twenty-acre rubber estate, a well-furnished house for accommodation and a two-storeyed building by the side of the main road for running the business? No one would be here in his native place who did not see, at least, that two-storeyed building with a plank-board, announcing in black and white letters 'St. Joseph Financiers'.

Though the dawn was gloomy and misty, and the chill wind was blowing against his face, Joseph Rich strode from the church towards his bank in perfect serenity. In fact, he had gone to the church thoroughly worried about those 'blade-companies' that flourished everywhere like mushrooms, threatening his own banking business. But, while praying at the church, he was really consoled by the verse in the Lord's Prayer, 'Lead us not into temptation'.

When the priest had pointed out in his powerful sermon,

just after the Holy *Qurbana*, that it was only greed that led man to evil, Joseph Rich nodded piously and agreed to that truth. He remembered that it was greed that also provoked man to start blade-companies in every nook and corner of his native place.

Each and every word in the Easter-message delivered by that reverend priest at the church came into his mind. The message was based on the incident in which Satan led even Jesus into temptation. He tried to imagine himself as Jesus in the wilderness.

The priest had described very touchingly how Satan tried to tempt the hungry Jesus who had come to the wilderness just after a fasting of forty days and forty nights, by saying, "Command that these stones be made bread!" and "Cast thyself down and the angels' hands shall bear thee up!" and "If thou wilt fall down and worship me, all the kingdoms of the world and the glory of them will I give thee!" How striking was it when the priest, continuing his message, had said that Jesus had escaped from falling into such temptations and that we too should take care not to fall victim to worldly temptations!

With much solace he had gained from the Easter-message of his parish-priest, Joseph Rich walked with quick steps towards his private bank.

Easter service was a midnight ceremony and it finished very early in the morning when even the twilight of dawn was hardly visible. Moreover, a transparent mist was still hanging around the street. From a long distance, he could only see his two-storeyed bank building like a vague shadow.

From that distance itself, Joseph Rich noticed that someone was standing on the terrace of his bank. He, very cautiously, inched towards the courtyard, feeling that the strange person would be a thief.

In the dim twilight of the dawn, the figure of that stranger appeared to be very horrible and grotesque. That ugly fellow with tattered clothes, disheveled hair and tangled beard waved his hand like a familiar person and invited Joseph Rich with a gesture of his forefinger.

Very carefully, Joseph Rich climbed up the steps to the terrace, collecting all his courage to face whatever happened. That stinking, black figure laughed aloud, emitting spirals of smoke from his mouth. And Joseph Rich stood there motionless for a moment without knowing what to do next.

Suddenly, pointing his forefinger towards the east, that figure asked: "Do you see that?"

Joseph Rich looked towards the east. There, he saw that the young sun was rising up over the tea gardens and cardamom estates.

The figure, pointing his forefinger towards the west, again asked: "Do you see that?"

Joseph Rich looked towards the west. There, he saw vast paddy fields, lying under the thick blanket of mist, far beyond the limits of his eyesight, almost touching the horizon.

Then, that figure pointed his forefinger towards the north and asked him once again: "Do you see that?"

Joseph Rich looked towards the north. There, he saw large plantations of thickly growing rubber and cashew trees.

Lastly, pointing his forefinger towards the south, that figure whispered: "Do you see that?"

Joseph Rich anxiously looked towards the south. There, he saw big factories and multi-storeyed skyscrapers.

Then, Joseph Rich stared at that ugly, monster-like figure questioningly, for he expected yet another instruction. Once again that figure laughed aloud and said in a serious tone: "All these will I give thee, if thou wilt fall down and worship me."

Joseph Rich stood speechless for a moment and, then, looked around in ecstasy. His heart was thumping fast and he could not define his emotions. When he thought about the unexpected fortune at his very doorstep, his eyes filled with tears of happiness. Once again, he looked around unbelievably. The people, who had been partaking in the holy rites of Easter Sunday, were returning home in small groups.

Suddenly, with fear and reverence, Joseph Rich knelt down and prostrated before that ugly figure and kissed his dirty feet. The monster-like figure, after lifting him up with both his hands, took a matchbox from the folds of his loincloth and lighted a *big-beedi*. Then, offering that *big-beedi* to Joseph Rich, he said in a commanding tone: "Smoke it."

Receiving the *big-beedi*, as if accepting a holy sacrament, Joseph Rich inhaled two or three breaths of smoke. Within a few minutes, he felt that his bank building was suddenly changing into an imposing skyscraper.

Joseph Rich looked again and again towards the east, towards the west, towards the north and towards the south. He saw that the tea gardens, the rubber plantations, the cardamom estates, the paddy fields, the cashew groves, the big factories and numerous multi-storeyed skyscrapers were coming closer and closer towards him.

Jumping up and down with unlimited joy, he laughed aloud and roared: "Today onwards, all these are mine....and mine only!"

Epilogue: The death of Joseph Rich. Is it a murder or a suicide? The public opinion is that if the police cannot find an answer, the citizens' action-councils can. But according to the Right-wing opposition, it was the 'cut-throat or *blade policy*' of the Left-wing Government that sent a 'poor banker' to the abode of Yama, the God of Death.

Author's notes and comments: Blade-company is a nickname given to those private financing banks, which charge cut-throat interest on their loans, established in Kerala, a State in South India, where the Communist Party, for the first time in the world, came into power through ballot paper. Holy Qurbana is the Holy Mass or Service in an Indian Orthodox Church. Big-beedi is a nickname used in Kerala for a kind of small cigar made from a leaf and filled with ganja or marijuana. Action-councils are formed in Kerala by the members of the public, usually with the back-up of political parties, whenever some-one is murdered. These councils spread too many rumors about the murder so that even the police themselves will be in utter confusion. The Right-wing Government in Kerala sponsored private financiers and when the Left-wing Government came into power, their policy was against such cut-throat financiers. Blade-policy sarcastically refers to the policy of the Left-wing Government against these blade-companies.

3

A JASMINE ON THE BASIL-PLANT PEDESTAL

Our Sridevi, or Chiruthei as the privileged class distorted or slanged her name either in disgust or in fun, came storming into the courtyard of our old, ancestral joint-family-house, and dug out the soil from the basil-plant pedestal. She was trying to pluck out the crooked and withered basil plant by root and branch from the soil with which the consecrated, three-foot high platform was filled.

Those who saw her eagerness and frenzied enthusiasm in pulling out the basil plant would think that she had been planning the same for many months and had also been thinking how wonderful it would have been if a jasmine plant, that grew straight up to the sky, was planted in the place of the basil plant!

No doubt, the heartbreaking sobs of our dearest Manu, who was chained and shackled to both the concrete pillars on which the huge water tank was built, kindled a sort of fiery enthusiasm that encouraged and motivated her!

We, the women of the joint family, dumbfounded in utter bewilderment of her thoughtless action, were standing timidly in the inner cellar of that ancient family-house. We were really surprised by her courage, and wondered how she could dare to do such an insolent deed! To destroy a basil plant, which was planted, protected and watered every morning by the women of the family, was not a small thing! Perhaps, she might be taking it as a medicine to cure the illness of her paralyzed mother!

The head of the family, whom we all called Eldest Uncle, the supreme authority over all the members of this joint family, was walking to and fro along the verandah of the porch like a caged musk-cat! We were relaxed noticing that Eldest Uncle, being immersed in some deep thought, was not at all looking at the direction of Sridevi. However, he shivered in excessive anger and growled like a lion, and even heaved heavy sighs intermittently.

Sridevi was quite adamant and acted with clear determination. It was evident that she noticed the restlessness of Eldest Uncle! She, with a smile hidden on her lips, pulled out the basil plant with all its root-stock and kept it folded in her fist. Then she took a jasmine stem and planted it in the soil where the basil plant had been growing!

We felt as if we were in a magic circle. We watched her running away with the folded basil plant in her hand, towards her hut, outside the vicinity of our house.

A few among us were trying to say, with our forefingers on our noses: What! Just a girl from a low-caste family, a mere daughter of a low caste woman, and...and this much courage!

But most of us were appreciating her by saying in our minds: What's there to be surprised about? The reason is as clear as daylight! Doesn't more than half of the blood that flows through the veins of Sridevi belong to persons who were born and brought up in this great family? Couldn't she show the courage of this family who had ruled this country with all the powers to kill and to murder?

But with our mind's eye we were seeing many more things: Sridevi is not going to get our dearest Manu! Her jasmine plant will not blossom and give fragrance to all! Or, before such a thing happens, the concrete pillars of the huge water tank must crumble down! Then Manu, who lay chained to the pillars, will be crushed to naught! Sridevi will be drowned in the flood water that rushes out of the tank! She and her hut together with her mother who lay paralyzed on a sack-cote inside the hut will be washed away forever! And we are damn sure about these...!

Manu was standing impatiently under the water tank, waiting to hear the sound of Sridevi's footsteps. Wrath burned in his eyes, for the springs of tears had already dried in them! Instead, one could see in those eyes, the flames of indignation and hatred towards the whole world! It seemed that he was acquiring and accumulating more and more energy from the roars and shouts of Eldest Uncle.

We, the humble women of the family, knew nothing, and were innocent about the nocturnal activities of the male members. All these should have been considered earlier! Yes, these so-called great uncles of this ancient family should have realized it, before they went to share the warmth of the low-caste women! Nobody could do miracles at the last moment, and the persons who ate salt must drink water!

All these years, we had been living in suffocation of this inner cellar of the ancestral house. These so-called uncles always boasted that nothing would happen to this great family when we, the unhappy women, cursed them! We were all mute and silent to the extreme! But no one could measure the depth of our real feelings!

We spent our sleepless nights alone in these cellars of the house, hearing the pit-pat of the out-pouring rain! The male members of the family went in search of the warmth of hard bodies! Our soft bodies might have become cold and lifeless due to their lack of love and self-respect! During those cold nights, we all cursed them in utter helplessness and agony. Fire of revenge was burning in our hearts all these years! Those arrogant uncles who did not care for the tears of the poor women of the family! What happened to them....? Where did they all go....in the passage of time?

Looking through the window of our cellar, we could see our dearest Manu struggling to break his chains. We, the women of this family, were directing our mental energy towards that cream of our family: Let him break his shackles! Let him bring Sridevi into this cellar of the ancestral house! Then only, our tears will become valuable! Then only, our words will acquire power....!

Not only our curses but also the curses of the low-caste women would have directed towards this ancestral house! In the hut, Sridevi's mother might be struggling to take her last breath: Where is the great Uncle who came years ago into this hut by midnight to share the warmth of my body and to sleep by my side? The air in this hut is too heavy to breathe! Ah, now the door is opened and a gale of coolness enters...! Is it the ghost of some great uncle who opens the door and steps into the hut....? Or is it Sridevi....?

The smell of the Krishna-basil plant might be piercing her nostrils, once again reminding her, the courtyard of the great family house! She might be feeling the sap of the basil plant flow through her veins, spreading all over her body! The sound of the footsteps of Sridevi who ran out of the hut was dissolving itself into the heavy breathing of the old woman....!

Our dearest Manu was pulling hard at the chains! The pillars of the water tank began to swing. We, the women of the family, foolishly calculated and visualized many things: The very next moment itself, our dearest dream of a Manu will be crushed under the huge water tank.....! Our greatest dream of 'a Sridevi' will be drowned in the flood-water of the crumbled water tank....! Her mother will be washed away in the flood of time like a nightmare! And we, the foolish women of this joint family, will live in this cellar for ever and ever....with no hope for escape!

Then, suddenly, we saw it through the window of our cellar! The concrete beams of the water tank broke and fell down! They fell on the chains of our dearest Manu, breaking the chains and freeing him! Within a split-second, he slipped away and saved his head from the heavy burden of the water tank! Sridevi, being completely exhausted, ran towards our dearest Manu and stuck to his chest! The crushed Krishna-basil plant, which she had been keeping in her hand, fell down from her grip!

We, the women of the family, cried aloud in panic when the water from the huge tank rushed towards our ancestral house! Into the mouth of Eldest Uncle, who stood agape without knowing what to do, mud and water rushed in! The wooden cellar of the house floated on the flood-water, carrying us, the women of the joint family!

We pulled Sridevi and our dearest Manu into the cellar. Our eyes scaled the area to find the hut of Sridevi's mother. We could not find it until the flood-water decreased its force. At last, when the flood subsided and when our cellar settled on the ground, we again began to look for the hut of Sridevi's mother. Later, we realized that our cellar was settled over the hut of that low-caste woman. In fact, the hut and our cellar became one and the same!

And there, in the courtyard of the great ancestral house, we saw the pedestal for black Krishna-basil plant undamaged by the flood! But, in the place of the basil plant, there was growing in its soil a jasmine plant, to blossom and to spread fragrance to all.....!

Author's notes: A three-foot high, square pedestal or basement, filled with soil, is kept in the courtyard of ancestral Hindu houses for growing a basil plant, as a symbol of grace. At first, my idea was to make my heroine plant a 'koovala' plant, the favorite of Lord Shiva, in the place of the basil plant, the favorite of Lord Vishnu; but she slipped away from my control and preferred a jasmine plant which is universal and free from religious discrimination! The Ancient Hindu religion was corrupted when Aryans came and established the caste system. In earlier days, it was based on occupations but, later, degraded into racial discrimination like apartheid.

4

IS TIGER A MAN-EATER BY NATURE?

It is quite natural that when you read this title of my short story, your mind may wander along the Kumaon jungle-villages of the Himalayas where once the man-eating tigers freely moved and where the great European hunter Jim Corbett created a new saga of their elimination.

If short story, like poetry, is a spontaneous overflow of powerful feelings recollected in tranquility, please do bear with me till I complete the description of the situation that inspired me to write this so-called story. Last evening, my father and I were walking down the road from Pithuragarh to Dharchula, two towns in the Kumaon district of Uttar Pradesh, and we stopped near a pedestal erected as a monument by the side of the road. The inscription on the stone read that it was the spot where the legendary Jim Corbett shot down one of the notorious man-eaters of Kumaon. Of course, one could read the details of that incident in his book 'The Man-eaters of Kumaon'.

My father also pointed out very proudly that, years later, it was his friend Mr. Gilbert who followed the steps of Jim Corbett and saved the rustics of Kumaon from the bloody fangs of the man-eaters. For a moment, the words 'Tiger' and 'Man-eater' made a sort of frenzied dance in my mind and helped me to dig out the following true story which I had buried in the depth of oblivion.

It all happened many, many years ago. I brought home the protagonist of my story from the house of a distant relative of mine, keeping that tiny creature in a plastic basket with sufficient air-holes, and covering the basket with a towel in order to hide it from the greedy eyes of the conductor of the government transport bus in which I had traveled[1]. The members of my family, including myself, named that black puppy 'Tiger' just because of our good intention that it should grow up into a fearless tiger-like dog. And never did we wish even in our remote dreams that he would become a man-eater!

We must admit the fact that our Tiger was at first very obedient and respectful to the members of our family. As it was described in the old nursery book, when the master returned home, he would waggle his tail, growl and murmur with love and when strangers came, he would bark aloud and make much fuss to attract our attention.

While we were taking our dinner, we used to throw pieces of cooked meat at him and he smacked his mouth, swallowing each and every bit of it quite deliciously. If bones were given to him, he would lick them or crack and suck the juice in such a way that our mouths filled with saliva. He ran and galloped around us as if to show that he was doing his duty honestly and punctually. Unfortunately, we were a bit late to know that he also was tempted by the contemporary diseases of indiscipline and disobedience.

One day, while playing in the courtyard, my son caught him by the tail for fun and, perhaps for more fun, he nibbled lightly and playfully at his finger. Hearing the screams of my son, I rushed towards him, and saw our darling Tiger lovingly lick away the blood that oozed out from a small scratch-like cut on my son's finger.

I stood bewildered for a moment, thinking over the horrible

consequences that would occur if a member of the canine or feline family tasted human blood! Of course, then I was reading Jim Corbett's The Man-eaters of Kumaon!

As days passed, I noticed some changes in the habits of our pet-dog Tiger. That didn't mean that he became mad or began to bite people in and out of our house! Without beating around the bush, should I say that I saw in his nature certain real drawbacks or shortcomings which we would not expect from a domestic dog. Of course, there was no decrease in his love and fidelity towards us or in the usual display of his courage.

First of all, forgetting all the etiquette of a domestic dog, during the daytime, he began to sleep like a wooden log! I really felt proud of this son of a Kumbhakarna[2], and appreciated him in my mind, thinking of his sincerity and hard work in properly protecting our house with his nightly patrols.

I became so furious when I found evidences that during the nighttime, instead of watching the gates of our house, he was lying at a remote corner of our land property. However, when I realized that he had been trying to break one or two bones, perhaps thrown out from the slaughterhouse, I did not do anything to him, respecting his canine instinct, but simply picked up those bones, made a deep pit and buried them. Why should we punish that dumb creature, I thought, instead of blaming those careless butchers who threw out bones here and there in the vicinity of poor domestic dogs?

The following day too, he brought two longer pieces of bones. The peculiarity in the shape of those bones frightened me, as they were not the bones usually found near butcheries. However, before anybody came to know about the incident, I buried them in a pit. But, the next night too, Tiger brought a cluster of bones; to be exact, it was the palm of a human being!

By then, the way things went was very clear to me. Tiger had turned into a man-eater! I felt dizziness and sat down in utter confusion.

Well! Near our land property, there was a cemetery belonging to a particular Christian denomination, the members of which did not care to build tombs for their dead; for they thought that such concrete structures would be an impediment for the dead to resurrect during the second coming of Jesus. To cut short a long tale, I understood that, for the previous few days, a dead body recently buried in that cemetery was the dinner of our Tiger!

Of course, I knew that the second stage of every man-eater was to catch, kill and eat live human beings. Before Tiger launched the second part of his operation, I bought a strong chain and locked him in the kennel. But, by that time, three or four sores had appeared on the body of Tiger, the sores that would appear on the body of dogs that eat rotten flesh; of course, ash from the fireplace was the best cure for similar rashes on dogs.

One should see the expression of cruelty on the face of Tiger, as he had been chained unexpectedly! When he saw me passing by the kennel, he stared at me like a werewolf; and snarled and growled at me like a wild dog. There was a sort of greed and hatred shadowed in his eyes; the intention to jump at me and tear me into pieces at the very next opportunity. Even my bones to their marrow turned numb with fear, when he stared at me with the silence of helplessness.

Two days later, I was waiting on the other side of the road for the line-bus that went to the city. Suddenly I saw Tiger, after breaking its iron-chain, was rushing towards me with the strong intention to attack and kill its arch-foe.

Soon a car, with European tourists, came fast and hit our Tiger away from me with a big 'bang' sound. The tourist car disappeared at the bend of the road leaving the lifeless body of our Tiger by the side of the road.

Even today I could remember the face of that European who had driven the car that killed our Tiger. For a moment, I wished to believe that his name was Jim Corbett, as he had killed our Tiger, the man-eater! But such a blunder would have happened even to you if you had been in my place! Therefore, should I not thank Jim Corbett for this story?

Author's notes: 1. In Government Transport buses, every living creature must have a ticket and, therefore, the villagers stealthily carry chickens, puppies and kittens in their plastic bags! 2. Kumbhakarna is a character in the epic Ramayana who used to sleep continuously for six months; it is a nickname for those who sleep longer.

5

THE REBIRTH

Realizing that it was very difficult to take a clear decision about the future, although the degree certificate was gained with a praiseworthy grade, that former student of mine came to me and asked me in a rather urgent but polite manner: "Sir! Tell me what should I do now?"

I was really attracted by his enthusiasm and sincerity. How many students are wasting away their days without getting proper advice on planning their future? No doubt, this young man is a model for our jobless generation and an asset for our nation, I thought.

As one among those college professors who showed no miserliness in doling out advice, I said: "Ours is a rubber city, full of rubber gardens, rubber tappers, rubber merchants, rubber factories, rubber products and, of course, rubber people. The whole city works like rubber, it extends when you pull and shrinks when you release and returns to its former position! So, it is better to start some sort of an industry or business that is related to rubber."

"But we must be careful about one thing," I continued. "Once we become a member of that rubber organization, we must adapt to that profession and become one with it! For example, suppose you want to start a rubber business! First of all, you must become a subscriber to one of the popular rubber magazines, flourishing like weeds in every nook and corner of this rubber country. Then, read everyday, the rubber news that comes in the rubber dailies! Make an evaluation of the rubber market. You must always update your rubber knowledge! Make studies on the fluctuations in the rubber price, the details on rubber export and rubber import, on rubber stock and rubber duties and rubber taxes, the government decisions on rubber control, etc. We should talk, read and think only about rubber....!"

Suddenly, that clever former student of mine interrupted me, as if he had taken a strong decision: "Sir! I understood what you are driving at! You mean that our talking, reading and thinking must be rubberized! And our body, mind and soul must turn into rubber! I understood every word of your advice in its full spirit. Thank you very much, Sir!"

He bowed his head with respect, walked out of the room and rolled on through the corridor. Then, I saw him move away along the street, hopping and jumping like a rubber ball....! Bhumm! Bhumm! Thud! Bhum! Thud! Bhumm! Bhumm....!

Author's note: The Malayalam translation of this story, with the caricature of a rubber-man, appeared in the Baselius College Annual, 1996.

6

LIQUOR TRAGEDY OR THE DIRECTION OF A MURDER

For how many years did our great sages say that liquor was mere poison and its drinking was sheer sin! Yet, it was quite sad that the number of persons who were addicted to liquor and met with untimely death was increasing day by day. And wasn't our story itself an excellent evidence to prove how addiction to liquor made people slave to other bad habits and how it led our society towards many an utter tragedy?

Like that of any other young men, it had been our humble desire to show our faces at least in a single cinema. And that was the only reason why, when a director who had won national awards for two of his films, offered a chance to act in his forthcoming feature film, we gratefully accepted it. Of course, we knew the risk of acting in an award film[1] directed by crazy directors!

At the shooting site, together with us, there were so many young persons who also desired to show their faces at least in a single film. Most of them, whether employed or unemployed, had come there after paying a sufficiently good amount to the director. Of course, in those days, acting in films and reading pulp literature had become an addiction like any other drugs!

The reception given by local citizens and other comrades to

a political leader who had recently won the election was the scene to be shot. In this scene, there was no dialogue for us, as its sound recording, the whistling, jeering and howling of the citizens as well as the shouting of slogans appropriate to the scene had been already done and kept ready for playing at the time of shooting.

A very famous comedian who had won a number of national awards for acting in films was doing the role of the political leader. We, who did not know even the 'a-b-c' of acting, memorized the scene thoroughly and blindly obeyed all the suggestions made by the director.

Sipping Scotch whisky, drop by drop, with soda at times and without soda at other times, the director caressed his long disheveled hair and pulled at his beard as if to stir his imagination. Then he said in a dragging tone, 'Just like my other two films, this also will be an award winning film. In fact, my film will be an experiment in realism or, rather, in naturalism. Therefore, what I need is not your artificial action because that would spoil the originality of my story. In short, what you are going to do in this film is not 'acting' but 'living'.

When the director's 'alcoholic rite'[2] almost came to an end, it was our turn. The waiters began to serve cheap quality 'rum', the so-called people's drink, to the leading actor, subordinate actors and persons like us who were supposed to have some influence on the director.

Of course, at first, we felt a sort of grudge against the system of keeping Scotch whisky as the monopoly of the director. However, we felt relieved and honored, noticing that most of the people, who came wearing white khaddar clothes[3] to act as citizens and supporters of the political leader, had to be satisfied with mere local arrack.

When everybody got boozed, the director raised his inebriating voice and said, "Now, let's start shooting the scene.

Once again I remind you that you are not supposed 'to act' but 'to live'. Don't raise your head and look straight at the camera or at the director. Do things as if there's no camera in front of you. Now, listen to the description of the scene: With great rapture and festivities, people garland the political leader, raise him on their shoulders, dance in a frenzied manner and carry him towards that sand-pile. Then all of you, standing around the political leader, will shout victory to him and he, afterwards, will express his vote of thanks to the citizens and supporters. Remember one thing; as film is insufficient for two 'takes', please make the scene a success in the first 'shot' itself by using your reason, talent and maximum efforts. OK? Ready? Start!"

Suddenly, a person came with a board on which the number of the scene was written and held it in between us and the camera and made the sound 'clap'. By that, together with the recorded sound, our jeering, howling and shouting as well as slogans and calls of 'victory' began to fill the atmosphere. We garlanded the political leader, raised him to our shoulders and began to dance in a frenzied manner.

Owing to intoxication, though we found it very difficult even to stand on our legs, we carried that extraordinarily fat political leader on our shoulders for some time and, then, threw him up in the air, caught him in our hands as he came down and, at times, when our hands could not hold him, he slipped down and fell on the ground. Ignoring the objections of the main actor, we raised him again and threw his heavy body up in the air and tried to catch it in our weak hands. And thus, the jubilant group moved towards the sand-pile. Of course, all this happened due to our Dutch courage which we regretted later.

We really felt hard to move forward as and when we reached the sand-pile. Our legs were losing their grip on the ground as the sand under our feet slipped away, and some of us even fell down flat. Somehow we managed to take the political leader to the top of the sand-pile and made him sit there.

Of course, the intoxicated actor who played the role of the political leader tried to escape from our hands in a semi-conscious manner by slipping down from the sand-pile. We all knew that it was the golden opportunity for us to impress our dear director and, therefore, we strongly determined to keep him there at the top of the sand-pile at any cost.

As somebody suggested, we decided to make a pit at the top of the sand-pile and place the political leader in the pit so that he could not slip down. Even then, many of us standing around him were shouting, without any sense of time or place, 'victory' to the political leader.

Soon four or five persons managed to climb up to the top of the sand-pile and began to make a pit with their hands. As our heads swung with intoxication, neither the pit-diggers nor we the bearers of the political leader noticed that the pit was a bit too deep for the purpose.

Then, we all lifted our leader up above our heads with loud jeering and shouting, and placed him with a 'thud' sound in the pit. But, as he was pretty intoxicated and out of balance, instead of sitting in the pit, he stretched his hands and legs, and lay flat in the pit. And certain naughty persons among us did not hesitate to push sand down into the pit.

Why should the event be unnecessarily much elaborated? While we were all howling and jeering and shouting victory to the political leader, that great comedian, who had been acting as the political leader, was suffocating under the sand!

The director, sitting at a far distance, could not understand, at first, what really was happening among the crowd. Then, realizing the seriousness of the situation, he walked towards us shrieking, "Cut! Cut!"

But some of our intoxicated comrades caught him too,

raised him over their shoulders and began to dance in a frenzied manner. Though he shrieked, "Cut, cut; cut, cut!' in an intoxicated tone, his voice drowned in the noise of our raptures.

Then, one of my friends who knew a bit of English whispered in my ears with a sort of guilty conscience, "Our dear director is asking us to cut the political leader into pieces. Alas! I forgot to bring even my penknife. Now, my fear is whether the film would lose its originality!"

Suddenly we heard a vehicle come and put its brake with a screech, and many of us began to run helter-skelter, crying, "Police, police; run and hide!" The revelry came to a standstill and, then and there, our intoxication turned icy cold and we realized the seriousness of the situation.

Not even wasting a single second, we too ran out so fast that we never felt our legs touching the ground! However, those people who were simply watching the shooting, stood there as statues, as they thought that it was all merely a part of the scene in the feature film.

Only the director and the policemen stood there bewildered. The director burst into tears like a grief-struck madman and began to remove the sand with his bare hands. The policemen, at first, thought that he was crazy, and blamed his boozing. Any intoxicated man would do such silly things!

Soon the director pulled out a leg from the sand and, only then, did the policemen realize the seriousness of the situation. All of them together pulled out that famous comedian, who had been acting as the political leader, from the sand-pit. But, by that time, he had breathed his last!

While participating in his funeral procession, we all sobbed bitterly, cried silently and wiped our tears either secretly or explicitly.

Months later, the court awarded the verdict deciding to

'hang till death' our dear director for crimes like culpable homicide, its abetment and its direction. In the absence of proper evidence, the court acquitted all of us and we consoled ourselves murmuring, "It's always better if one man dies for the sake of all others."

Didn't you understand at least by now how liquor was a menace to the individual as well as to society and how the addiction to liquor brought forth an utter tragedy?

Author's notes: 1. The term 'award film' was generally used to laugh at experimental cinema taken by certain bohemian directors and shown only before award committees or viewed only by the so-called intelligentsia. 2. In India, before the shooting of a film begins, there will be a 'puja' or rite, a ceremony to get the blessings of God. 3. Mahatma Gandhi recommended 'khadhar' or home-spun clothes for politicians, but later it had become a symbol of hypocrisy and corruption.

7

FATE OF PEOPLE IN THE LAND OF COCONUT-TREES

After a journey of about one hundred miles from our village, my wife and I were in our capital city, just to visit the most famous temple there, to make our obeisance before the deity, an incarnation of Lord Maha Vishnu, and to snatch for us his blessings!

After getting the permission of the half-naked porter of the temple, my wife entered the abode of the Lord. And I stood outside the temple like the squirrel that lost its nut! For they did not allow me to enter the temple as I was covering the nakedness of my chest with a shirt! Men should not cover their chests before the Lord, they pointed out. Was there anything obscene on my chest, I wondered.

I remembered that once a great saint of this country had called this part of the nation a 'mad-house'! Great men usually realized the secrets of our hearts! Though outwardly we pretended to be the most civilized, inwardly, due to our sheer hypocrisy, we were the worst kind of fanatics who never accepted facts!

As a traveler, I had toured all over the country and had visited almost every major temple, mosque and church outside my state, and it was for the first time that I was asked to strip off before entering a holy building! I took it for granted that we were all naked in the eyes of the Lord Almighty but was it a reason for us to continue ourselves to be barbarously fanatic on such issues? And we were the citizens of a state that had declared literacy of ninety-nine percent, waiting at the threshold of the twenty-first century!

I stood outside the portals of the temple quite disappointed. For a moment, I thought about the whims and fancy of our Gods! While the Indian God likes to see the half-naked bodies of His devotees, the Arabian God likes to see His devotees completely wrapped in clothes! While the God of Israel doesn't like foot-wears, the European God never likes His devotees take off their shoes! The Indian God likes His worshippers fall flat on the ground in obeisance; the Arabian God likes His worshippers fall on their knees; the European God prefers His believers sit on their chairs! The God who doesn't allow His devotee stand with folded hands to greet aged people or touch the feet of his great grandfather or great grandmother insists him to fall on his knees and kiss the hands of a sheikh, emir or khalipha! What a strange paradox! In short, I was on the horns of a dilemma whether to expose my bone-cage of a chest to gain entrance into the temple or not!

Soon somebody touched me on the shoulder and I turned back to see a young man with a strange bluish complexion. I noticed that he had a peacock-feather on the crown placed on his head and a flute tucked in the folds of his loincloth. His apparel was that of a dancer and I thought that he was there to get the blessings of the Lord before his '*arangettam*' or the first performance on a stage. Of course, he was wearing no shirt!

He expressed his sympathy at my predicament and said that he belonged to that place and was watching this ancient African tradition everyday! He consoled me and told me the strange story of this uncivilized practice.

"There was a time when gods loved to see the naked chests of both men and women!" He began.

I could understand that part of the story. In ancient days, there were no shirts or blouses and people entered the temple bare-chested. For the same reason, our gods and goddesses were also presented on paintings and sculptures as bare-chested! Moreover, while painting the pictures of our gods, the artists were very particular in blending feminine and masculine features on the same god! One could not see an Indian god with a hairy chest! Naturally, that might be the reason why our gods desired to see the hairy chests of our men! Otherwise why should these so-called protectors of gods have asked me to remove my shirt and pants before entering the temple?

I could not blame those kings or priests or other temple-folks or, even, those common believers! For in this land of the coconut-trees, while women grew taller, men remained dwarfs, physically and mentally! How prophetic was that great man of yesteryears who called this land a lunatic asylum!

"And in those days, women of this place had no 'bulgings' or swollen parts on their chests," he continued. "For this land was full of coconut-trees that carried heavy burdens of coconut-bunches. And we proudly called this part of the country the Land of Coconut-trees."

I could understand that part of the story also. Here, speaking botanically, there might be a lot of coconut-trees, and speaking zoologically, a few human beings! And that was the reason why men and women went to temples bare-chested for the *darshan* or the holy glimpse of the Lord!

"But without mammary glands, called breasts by our natives, how could their children survive?" I asked him, with a sort of distrust in his story.

"Then the children of this land grew up drinking coconut water and eating tender coconuts....!" he said in a dreamy voice.

Just imagine! As usual, the believers came for the holy *darshan* and the priests performed their rites and ceremonies. Then too, gods sat, just like on these days, in their shrines, quite silently and pretending that they did not see anything! And everything went peacefully and beautifully!

He said: "As things went on like this, unfortunately, one fine morning, all the coconut-trees of this land were infected by a disease called 'windfall' and, thereby, the leaves of the coconut-trees began to whither away and the coconuts began to fall down before it was time! As coconuts were the only identity of this land, the women of this land came forward and volunteered to grow coconuts on their chests....!"

"Of course, in all critical situations, the women of this land came forward with their inborn sense of dedication and sacrifice, and saved the face of our men. Even at times, the prudence of these women saved our men from the disgrace regarding the fatherhood of their children!"

My friend continued: "Thanks to the sacrifice made by the women of this land that the priests performed their religious duties by drinking coconut water and eating tender coconuts.....!"

I could understand the rest of the story! As time passed, the priests might have declared coconuts as inevitable things for all religious rites and rituals. Moreover, our innocent women considered that it was their moral obligation to show the presence of coconuts on their chests when they entered the temple. And in the passage of time, the coconuts on the chests of our women were transformed into breasts and, yet, the priests continued to enjoy the sight, convincing the women that they were not breasts but mere coconuts!

"It was during that time," my young friend continued, "that the king of this land, who imposed taxes on anything and everything that grew bigger and larger, issued an edict to collect 'breast tax' from women. But one of the courageous women of this land, one day, severed her breasts with a kitchen knife and placed them on a banana leaf and gave it to the tax collector....!"

Of course, such an incident would have compelled the authorities to put a full stop to the breast tax! It was natural that the women of this land, who had a bit of the Amazonian spirit in them, did such courageous things! Or, being afraid of giving tax, the women of this land began to cover their chests to the disappointment of the priests! The women of this land soon realized the fact that their fertile breasts were sources of inspiration not for the gods but only for the priests! Our women covered their chests and entered the temple to have the holy *darshan* of the deity. Moreover, the king issued another edict declaring that the 'windfall' that affected the coconut-trees of this land was eradicated forever!

But....! My dear Holder of the Flute and Peacock-feather! Our women are lucky! And my wife entered the temple to have her *darshan* of the Lord! "What about me....?" I asked my blue-complexioned friend.

Taking out the flute from the folds of his dress, he played a divine tune, and as I stood there immersed in the mesmerizing effect of the music, he removed the flute from his lips and said to me with a cunning smile: "Well! It's a pity! Let's pray for another 'windfall'...!" He moved slowly to the back of the temple.

I could understand the rest of the story! We, the men of this land, who poured the spirit of revolution into these women, were forced to visit the temples without covering our chests! We were all dreamers while our women were quite practical in their day to day life. We were still dreaming that a day would come again, in which that horrible disease called 'windfall' would come back attacking the coconut-trees of this land, so that the leaves of the coconut-trees would wither away and the coconuts would fall down prematurely and, then, the men of this land also could come forward as volunteers to grow coconuts on their chests; and that the king would issue another edict to collect breast tax from them, and one among them would sever his breasts and offer it on a banana leaf to the tax collector, following which all other men would cover their chests, and that the priests would be disappointed as our men entered the temple covering their chests with shirts! Let their reverie come true! Amen!

I saw my wife coming out of the temple, after having her *darshan* of the Lord. I led her to the back of the temple as I wished to show her my blue-complexioned friend. I could not find him anywhere there, but saw the deserted peacock-feather lying on the ground, perhaps, fallen down from the crown of my storyteller.

I took that peacock-feather home with me and kept it in my diary, as a holy offering from the Lord, so that it would deliver more peacock feathers, as we used to believe when we were mere school children.

Author's notes: The holy glimpse of a deity is called *darshan*. Lord Krishna, with a peacock feather on his crown, is the incarnation of Lord Maha Vishnu.

8

THE STORY OF A SALE

Nobody was there in our village who did not know Butcher Kunjootty. In fact, he was not at all a butcher but a local animal dealer or a middleman who bought 'creatures' from the villagers and supplied them to the slaughterers. Of course, he had acquired a lot of characteristics of those dumb creatures due to his continuous acquaintance with them from his childhood onwards.

Kunjootty came out of his house and walked along the muddy road that crossed our village to the town, only at dawn or at dusk or at midnight and, at that time, our sheep, safely kept in their folds or sheds, would bleat aloud recognizing the smell of his body. Of course, it was natural if our sheep cried aloud feeling the odor of Butcher Kunjootty but why our domestic dogs howled at odd times was always a mystery for us, the villagers. And who did know where Kunjootty spent most of his time, day or night!

He always wore the same kind of *lungi*, with long stripes on dull gray color. No one had seen him wearing a shirt. He wore a green belt around his waist as if to keep his *lungi* tight to its place. There were two pockets for his belt, one on the left side filled with currency notes to buy sheep and the other on the right with *beedi*, the local leaf-cigar. And the matchbox would be kept in a fold of the *lungi*, near the backbone, just above the belt.

He used to fold his *lungi* to double it and, with the second part tied tightly around the waist almost completely covering the belt. He raised his *lungi* and folded it so high that any person could see the lower part of his underwear from behind. And these were only a part of his outward show!

To say about the physical aspects of Kunjootty, his height was more than six and a half feet. Yet he appeared only as tall as any one of us due to his hunch, or a curve of his backbone from the neck down to the waist. People used to say that this hunch came only because he always stooped to assess the price of the sheep and, after buying the sheep, pulled them with a rope tied around its neck towards the slaughter house.

His body was as strong as that of a stone statue. The color of his body was that of half-fried coffee-powder. The skin on his lean face was so tightly covered over the bones that anyone would say that he had a mummy's appearance. His hands were so long that the thin, skeleton-like fingers on the palms reached below the knees. It appeared as if muscles, veins and arteries climbed up twining around the bones of his hands and legs. In short, Kunjooty, except for the hunch of the backbone, was like the picture of the man in the chart brought into the classroom by the science teacher to teach human muscular system.

On the animal-market-day, one could see Kunjootty everywhere! On other days, we used to see him at odd times, as buying ganja *beedi* from that notorious Moideen's shop, or as licking opium bits sitting in the tea-shop of our grand-old Opium-Pillai or as relaxing in the hut of Mistress Annama, sipping her illicit liquor. We noticed with surprise that he drank only arrack, the locally brewed liquor, and even if he entered a toddy-shop, he drank not even a drop of toddy but only ate a plate or two of cassava with spicy fish curry.

Whatever people had been saying about him, one thing was

damn sure: every individual and every sheep in our village knew Kunjootty, but Kunjootty knew none of us but only our sheep! Owing to the curve of his backbone, he walked always looking down on the road but he assessed the price of each and every sheep in our village. No doubt, if anybody bought a sheep at a higher price than what he assessed, the buyer would meet with a loss!

Kunjootty, in his area of work, was always honest and he neither changed his word nor the price he offered for a 'creature', whether sheep, ram, cow or bull. As this habit was not common among animal dealers, a sort of blind faith in Kunjootty developed among us, the villagers. With a single observation, he could assess the price of any animal and there was no need for bargaining with him.

Moreover, as Kunjootty was concerned, unlike other animal-dealers, the question of credit never did come up, neither in selling nor in buying. He fixed a sale only after giving the price then and there. All these things were only a prologue to prepare your mind from a shock when you heard the story of a sale made between Kunjootty and myself.

For the previous month, I was planning to sell the only sheep I had. Though for many a time I sent this sheep in the company of rams, she failed to conceive and I found her quite profitless to feed. Moreover, since much changes had come in my wife's lifestyle, for example, no more firewood fetching as gas-cooking started, no more manual clothes-washing as electric washing machine was bought, no more drawing of water from the well as Municipal water connection was extended to the village and so on, she did not like to walk under jackfruit trees and collect leaves for the sheep and, unfortunately, there was no electric machine invented for that purpose! She kept on nagging me to sell the useless sheep to some slaughterers. But all these days, I did not get time to inform the matter to Kunjootty or any other dealer in animals.

One day, after a heavy lunch, I was lying on an easy-chair in the drawing-room, reading the newspaper. Gradually, I slipped into my noon-time siesta as it was my habit. Suddenly, Kunjootty approached me, as if from nowhere, and asked me without any formal introduction, "Are you selling the 'creature' that stands under that jackfruit-tree?"

By the way, Kunjootty never used the words 'sheep', 'goat', 'ram', 'lamb', 'cow', 'calf' or 'bull', instead he used the word 'creature' to represent any animal. It was a technical term commonly used among animal-dealers, for they considered only the 'meat-value' of an animal.

I was very happy to see Kunjootty so unexpectedly; as if you were looking for an essential medicinal-creeper and,suddenly, you found the herb tangled on your leg! A sale at the door without any botheration or waste of time! I told him very fluently, of course with a bit of exaggeration, that the so-called 'creature' in my custody had much meat, and its mother produced much milk and so on.

But, without heeding to my sincere descriptions, he asked me in a rough voice, "Are you ready to sell it for three hundred rupees?"

I expected only a maximum of two hundred rupees for my sheep and so, hearing the good price 'three hundred', I immediately agreed to sell it. Moreover, I had heard from my neighbors that if one bargained over the price of a sheep with Kunjootty and, thereby, the sale was aborted, he would go straight to the sheep as if to check whether he could increase the price, and raise it up in the air holding by its backbone as if to estimate the weight of its meat, so that the poor creature's growth would come to an end forever!

Kunjootty would not talk too much, especially, while dealing with serious business matters. He took out three hundred-rupee notes and placed them in my hands and, without uttering a single word, went out of my house. Kunjootty was always like that; once the sale was fixed, he would not waste his time!

I casually counted the currency bills, folded them with a yawn and safely kept them in the fold of my *lungi*. Then, I turned to a more comfortable position in my easy-chair to resume my noon-time siesta.

A few minutes later, hearing the loud crying of my wife from under the jackfruit-tree, I ran towards the spot. On the way, I noticed my sheep standing in its shed, bleating in an exclusive tone to express its hunger. In fact, my wife had gone down to the jackfruit tree only to collect the fallen leaves for the sheep.

At first, I thought that my wife was crying because of the grief in parting with her pet sheep. But when I saw the shocking sight under the jackfruit tree, I felt my whole body turn numb. Without any expression of sentiments on his face, Kunjootty was pulling hard on the rope that was tied round the neck of my wife!

I shivered with anger and my words scattered from out of my mouth, "Sirrah! You...! What the hell are you doing?"

He replied without any emotion on his face, "Didn't I fix the price for the creature standing under the jackfruit-tree, and pay the amount? Once the sale is fixed, Kunjootty won't change his word! Understand?"

His indifference and placid voice frightened me to the core. He pulled again on the rope that was tightened around the neck of my wife. His intention was to take the poor creature home, as he had paid its value. My wife cried louder and louder, and even cursed my cowardice. With all my strength, I tried to push away Kunjootty from my wife but my effort was as awkward as that of an ant trying to push down a rock from the mountain-top.

Suddenly, he raised his iron-like fist and struck me on my head. I fell down flat on the ground with a shriek. I felt as if I lost all my senses. While lying down in that semi-conscious state, I heard the waves of my wife's crying and sobbing beat against my ear-drums. The long, frightening, helpless crying....! Like the mournful bleating of the sheep that was dragged towards the slaughterhouse.....!

Author's notes: Lungi is a colorful dhoti or long household cloth, usually worn by men in South India. It is believed that the domestic dogs make long howling at odd times seeing Yama, the god of death. As I am getting older and older, the protagonist in this story haunts me frequently like an angel of death and, therefore, though I wrote it in 1982, I love this story still.

9

THE TRAGIC DEATH OF A PRIME MINISTER

It was, shall I say, just the foul-play of my bad fate that the whole responsibility of the Prime Minister's protection fell on my head and shoulders. Well, I could do almost every difficult job under the sun quite easily and single-handedly. But to protect the life of a Prime Minister, especially of a person who was elected to rule a country like that of ours, was really a headache! And if that person's profile, character and habits were similar to that of mine…! Howzzaat!

In fact, the main reason to entrust me with such a responsibility was the similarity of my face with that of the Prime Minister. And for the same reason, his life as well as mine faced the same risk, and threats of the same danger. In other words, one could not ignore the possibility of our deaths, individually or together!

Things had really turned worse since the people of my country left their human faces and began to accept the faces of wild animals like lions, tigers and black panthers! Their roars and their long, sharp claws and their curved fangs – needless to say, all had spoiled the peaceful sleep with colorful dreams of the Prime Minister, and of mine as well!

I was neither a tamer of wild animals nor the protector of wildlife! I was only the Chief Protector of the Prime Minister; a simple chance I got by the grace of seniority! I was a person ready to sacrifice my own valuable life to save the Prime Minister's life. Never was I so reluctant to place my life at such a risk! But don't blame me when I say that it is quite meaningless to die without any genuine reason! As if in the case of an elephant, the capital amount is safe, whether a prime minister, or even a bishop, lives or dies! But what about my death? I would be pushed to that mass of the unknown 'dead-millions'! I would become one among those thousands who perished every day in this country, of whom nothing was marked or remembered; 'unsung and un-honored'! Yet, if a Prime Minister happened to die due to a fault in my calculations or a crack in my intelligence, though I might not be directly blamed, it would be a national tragedy and, at the same time, a personal tragedy for me too!

And that's why I felt totally confused when the Prime Minister decided to take a photograph, posing with the female and male artists of the country. I tried to convince myself that artists would not have that much cruelty to murder a handsome and good-looking Prime Minister! But in the case of artists and writers, the working of their brains is so obscure and strange that I burned the midnight oil over the means to protect the life of the Prime Minister. At last, with the help of our top-ranked scientists, we developed a special kind of cotton-strap which would resist anything that was solid, liquid, jelly or gas!

On the day of taking the photograph, I covered the whole body of the Prime Minister with that specially prepared cotton-strap, though, then, he looked like an astronaut ready for space travel! Or should I say it more clearly, our Prime Minister then looked just like how cartoonists drew the caricature of a comedian lying on a hospital-bed with all bones broken following a very serious accident!

Needless to say more, except for the two holes at the place of the eyes, the whole body of the Prime Minister, from top to toe, was covered with the cotton-strap of two-inch width. In short, once wrapping was over, he looked exactly like the dead body of a Jew before its burial! In order to cover the two holes in front of his eyes, I arranged a special kind of bullet-proof black goggles. Using my exclusive authority as a Special Protection Officer of the Prime Minister, I also warned the Prime Minister not to remove the goggles under any circumstance.

There were twenty artists with whom the Prime Minister had to sit for the photograph. Six of them were veteran artists and, so, I arranged seven chairs in a row so that the Prime Minister could sit in the middle and the senior artists could sit on either side of the Prime Minister, three on the left and three on the right.

There were seven beautiful female artists who were asked to stand on the carpet just behind the Prime Minister's row. Behind the female artists, seven male artists would stand on a bench, and it was the last row. Thus, I arranged the positions of the Prime Minister as well as of his guests in a very systematic way.

We had already checked the whole area, the chairs, the benches and the camera, with a metal detector. We made our security arrangements double-sure before the entrance of the Prime Minister. Then, the photographer was led to the arena under severe scrutiny.

Then, it was the turn for the artists to be checked. Those parts of the human body where there was the possibility of hiding destructive weapons and other explosives were brought under special observation.

The ladies of my squad checked the young male artists of the team. These women were not only experienced in their job but were also ready to volunteer to do such duties with great interest and enthusiasm.

A few young men of my squad, who were highly suspicious of anything and everything, competed among themselves to check, one after another, those young female artists whose breasts appeared to be highly explosive! In fact, all the members of the security staff were very suspicious about such extraordinary bulging or growths on their bodies.

After the necessary scrutiny and security checking, all the artists were brought one by one to the dais, and the security staff guided them to their respective places. They were asked to sit or stand in their deputed places. I moved towards the camera and the photographer to make a general survey or reconnoitering of the arrangements. After observing the whole arena, I warned them, with an air of authority, not to move their limbs unnecessarily or too swiftly or even their heads this way or that way, after the arrival of the Prime Minister.

When everything and everybody was ready, the Prime Minister came to the dais, completely cordoned and protected by the security staff. He sat on the chair reserved for him. The members of the security squad stood with their loaded guns, out of bound of the camera-eye.

The male and female artists tried to suppress their laugh while they looked at the odd figure of the Prime Minister who came to the dais like a silk-worm in its pupa stage, completely covered with the cotton-strap, except for his eyes, where there were two holes, and they too were covered with black goggles!

Unfortunately, I had informed the artists that there was nothing wrong in making a formal smile, just at the moment of taking the photograph. And, therefore, I did not take it seriously when the youngest female artist who stood just behind, by the left side of the Prime Minister's chair began to smile, showing her shiny and pearl-like teeth! It might be because she was the most beautiful among the artists that when she began to smile a sort of light or rather a halo spread from her, and I could consider it only as part of her exclusive beauty!

For a moment, I wondered how those dreamy Mongolian eyes, those plump, red Persian cheeks, that curly, black Dravidian hair and the wheat complexion of the Aryan origin blended in her so proportionately and perfectly!

The muscles on the faces of all the artists and others began to tighten and stretch as the photographer began to count slowly: One.....two......! Finally he said, 'three' and together with a flash of light, he took the photograph.

Immediately, the smile on the face of that beautiful female artist who stood by the left of the Prime Minister turned to a loud laugh and, in the voice of her laughter, the Prime Minister was so shocked that his black goggles, ejecting from his face, flew away, quite against my warning, and fell just in front of the camera! All these happened together and exactly at the same time that nobody could understand what actually was happening!

She continued to laugh louder and louder! It took some time for me to free myself from that quandary and understand what was actually occurring! By that time, her laugh, like any other infectious disease, began to spread, first to other female artists who stood near her, and then, to those intelligent male artists who stood behind her row! I felt that the waves of laughter that rose up around the Prime Minister would upturn his equilibrium and disturb his equanimity! Perhaps, the Prime Minister was also joining in the laughing of the artists and the intelligentsia, I thought.

Like a robot that lost its control due to some mechanical defect, the Prime Minister slowly stood up and began to wade a few feet! Gradually, he began to swing sideways and to shiver and vibrate! And then, he started producing some strange sounds!

At first, tears began to flow out of the holes that were in the place of his eyes, as if it were the result of his heavy laughing! Then, gradually, the flow of tears from the holes became more forceful! They seemed to be tears but, in fact, as I realized later, his body was melting and his liquid body was coming out through the holes which were the only openings in his bandaged body! Soon came out through those holes foam and bubbles, smoke and stench, and then, a sort of liquid or jelly with different bright colors! And the flow continued with an intermittent force...!

I stood there like a wooden statue without knowing what to do! I noticed that changes were also happening to that beautiful girl who had been incessantly laughing all through! I stood there wonderstruck, watching the muscles of her face tightening and stretching, her limbs turning leaner and longer like that of a skeleton, her teeth growing into long, curved fangs with blood dripping from them, and she was transfiguring into some sort of an alien creature....!

Gradually, smoke began to emit from her. As the other artists began to realize the emergency of the situation, they also stood stupefied. The sound of that beautiful girl's laugh began to echo and reverberate in the atmosphere. And her body began to emit smoke and sparks and flames and....and, soon, she turned into a jelly-like substance and disintegrated into nothingness....!

At the same time, changes also came to the Prime Minister's figure! The cotton-strap, with which his body was covered, shrank into a pile of cotton, loosening its knots. And, finally, it fell forward to the front of the camera, just like the black goggles! As a last attempt to save his life, I ran towards him and took him in my hands, but by that time, our dearest Prime Minister had turned into a tangled bundle of old rags!

Clutching on the rusted iron bars of the prison-cell, I

wondered why all these fools deliberately preferred to become Prime Ministers or Presidents!

Author's Notes: History is neither 'his story' nor 'her story' but the 'high story' or 'hi-story' of those who try to attain or retain power. Power, undoubtedly, is a drug that works sometimes as a cure but mostly as an intoxicant, leading its victims to strange hallucinations. The magnetic charm of power gives a sort of Dutch courage that induces or tempts people to walk into death by suicide or martyrdom; power is like fire into which termite-flies are drawn.

10

THE END OF AN EVANGELIST

And the evening and the morning were the third day!

Even then, he did not care to come down from the top of that jack-fruit tree! He was still clutching to the apex of the topmost branch of that tall tree, the only tree in his courtyard. It seemed that, from there, he was going to climb up the last step towards heaven! Like a wayside evangelist, he was shouting and calling out something like a biblical harangue, turning his head left and right and raising his forefinger or fist up in the air.

He might be imagining that he was addressing a large gathering! Of course, there was a large crowd, whom he could not see from that height, waiting under the tree, expecting the spectacular scene of his fall from the tree! In fact, they did not want to miss such an exceptional moment in their life!

His 'sermon on the tree' was sometimes in a language which everybody could understand and other times it was in a language which nobody could follow! Most of the time, he was only repeating those sentences which he had been speaking for the last two days. And he stood at the top of the tree as a link in between heaven and earth!

Every spectator knew that if he was not a mad man, he must be at least an ordinary mental patient, slightly abnormal or eccentric! And for that reason, the enthusiasm of the people, which they showed for the first two days, reduced considerably and, at last, the number of them dwindled into a few. And as a neighbor, how could I leave him alone, like others, in such a condition!

He continued to talk this and that, as if it were his daily routine for many years! Moreover, it seemed that he was preparing himself for a rebirth, as he was completely naked!

In appearance, he was a healthy and handsome young man. A thirty-five-year-old man with curly hair, wheat complexion and strong muscles! The jack-fruit tree stood in front of his thatched house and, due to his weight, the highest branch of the tree bent to the maximum and hung just above the main road, at the very middle of the street. The branch, on which he was sitting, swayed in the wind as if it would break at any moment. It seemed that, at any moment, he would definitely fall head downwards on the very centre of the street and die without getting time to breathe his last! And the people who stood on the road were waiting breathlessly for that unique and exciting moment!

On the street, below the swinging branch of the jack-fruit tree, stood a few employees of the Fire Force, who were experienced in so-called disaster management, engaged in making funny comments or smoking a lot of cigarettes. Though they were government employees, appointed for rescuing those in danger, they took it as a casual incident and were not bothered about the seriousness of it. Of course, they tried sincerely to bring him down from the tree for the first two days. But they had to cease their efforts as he had threatened to jump down from the tree. It seemed that they knew that under such circumstances, the only duty left for them was to take his dead body for post mortem to some mortuary in the government hospital, as and when he fell down.

Among the spectators, there were also a few lazy young

men, who regularly drew their unemployment allowance, impatiently waiting for the final catastrophe! People from the neighborhood had made their usual 'sightseeing' in the morning itself and had gone to their worksites. They might have consoled themselves thinking that they could see the same funny scene even when they returned from their work in the evening!

Sitting on the topmost branch of the jack-fruit tree, he said, as if it were a part of his mission: "O generation of vipers, who hath warned you to flee from the wrath to come? Is this not anything for you, who pass by this way! He that hath ears to hear let him hear! I love my wife more than anyone else! Only her, I took as my wife! Therefore, if others try to make her their wife, it's a sin! Amen!"

For a minute he stopped, looked around as if observing the reaction of his imaginary audience in the air, and continued: "You ask me where my wife is! She always works hard in my thatched hut. You say that she has no children because I am a lazy man! But how many priests come to my house and go out quite pleased! The voice of their chants reaches even to the top of this jack-fruit tree! While those who got at least two pounds, could double it, what shall I do, for I am a person who did not get even a single pound?"

His voice resounded in the atmosphere like the genuine lamentation of a bereaved man. And for the spectators, it was only a matter of mere fun and entertainment!

Even at that time, just like on the two previous days, I was walking to and fro along the verandah of my house, quite restlessly. How could I work with concentration or sleep peacefully when my neighbor was sitting at the top of a tree? Who could be able to care for even one's son or his mother when one felt a sort of vacuum in the mind?

For the last two days, neither voice nor smoke was coming

out of my kitchen! A sort of silence of the cemetery prevailed everywhere. Moreover, for the last two days, I was not hearing even the lisping of my son or the scolding of my wife; it might be because my attention was only on the man in the tree.

Earlier, from his thatched hut, his wife's intermittent laments had aroused my curiosity. But that too was ended and his hut too was drowned in a sort of mysterious quietness. And I was only aware of the smoke, of frankincense and incense sticks, that came out from his hut and strained into my house, spreading its fragrance everywhere.

Still the voice of his 'sermon on the tree' was coming down from the top of the jack-fruit tree: "Woe unto you, oh wives! Woe unto you, oh priests! Woe unto you, oh hypocrites who watch me from the roadside! Why don't you care for the smoke of frankincense that rises up from my hut? To what purpose is this waste? But all these are the beginnings of sorrow, for all these things must come to pass! Then, what's the use in running here and there, crying aloud, 'Oh Mountains, fall on us! Oh Caves, swallow us! Ye serpents, ye generation of vipers, how can ye escape the damnation of hell?"

In the violent enthusiasm of the oration, he slipped for a second his grip from the branch, arousing a cry of alarm from the spectators! One policeman was so nervous that he ordered him in an abusive language to come down from the tree. But the evangelist continued: "Verily I say unto you, this generation shall not pass, till all these things be fulfilled. And let him that on the treetop not go down into the house, neither enter therein, to take anything out of his house. He that hath ears to hear, let him hear!"

His voice was pregnant with sincerity and his words were full of integrity. It seemed that the fragrance that rose up from his hut drove me into some sort of a magic spell. As the workers of the Fire Force and those young men who drew unemployment allowance sat on the street engaged in smoking or talking on silly subjects, I slowly walked into that hut, in search of the source of the frankincense smoke.

At first, I could not feel the presence of any person in the hut. The door was not locked and so, without making any noise, I opened it slowly and peeped through the cleft into the room. It was a pretty large drawing room. A traditional oil lamp was burning dimly in the middle of the room and that was the only source of light though it failed to remove the darkness of the room. In front of the oil lamp, there was a flat mud-vessel filled with coal-embers over which pieces of frankincense emitted spirals of smoke. The room was filled with smoke of frankincense so that I was unable to see things clearly. Yet, I could feel the movement of a shadow somewhere at the extreme corner of the room.

Owing to my uncontrollable curiosity, I strained my eyes to see who or what was there! An old priest, wearing a long, black gown, stood there, and he was bending forward and backward over a bed, as if he were doing some ritual calisthenics. I noticed that the old priest, holding the seams of his gown stretched to sideways, was falling on the bed and, then after a moment, standing up erect, and repeated the same action again and again! And I stood there in utter bewilderment and surprise.

He was chanting some weird 'mantras' or enigmatic words and, at times, raised his hand and vibrated it in a ritualistic manner. Suddenly, I noticed that a boy was laid motionless on the bed, and the old priest's lips were touching the boy's forehead, chest and naval, one after the other. The boy's face was not clear as the old priest's long beard crawled over his body. I concluded in my mind that a kind of ancient, barbarous ritual was taking place there!

I opened the door a bit more and silently sneaked into the

room. The old priest was completely immersed in his ritual. I looked around the room and, suddenly, noticed that there was also another person, a woman, standing attentively by the side of the old priest.

She was a beautiful woman in her twenties and was wearing a long, red gown. Though her back was turned towards me, I soon realized that she was the wife of the evangelist who sat atop the jack-fruit tree. She stood there like an epitome of feminine beauty, like an example of anatomic perfection or like an invaluable marble sculpture created by some great Hellenic artists! Her long, red gown, completely wet with sweat or damp with oil, was tightly stuck to her body. It seemed that she too was participating in the ritual of the old priest, as she murmured certain strange words and showed certain mysterious gestures with her hands!

Soon, I found that there was a third person too in the room! At another corner of the room, a young woman was lying on a white carpet spread on the floor, as if she were the replica of the other woman. Only a white silk-shawl, as thin as the gush of a grey-mist, covered her body! She was lying there as if she was drowned in some spiritual ecstasy, and her whole body was smeared with some fragrant oil.

I moved towards them in order to see who that young woman was. I saw her smiling with her half-closed eyes, as if experiencing a wonderful dream in her sleep. Suddenly, a lightning flashed from the eyes of the young woman and a thunder struck inside my brain!

From that lightning, the smoking frankincense in the mud vessel caught fire; flames rose up from it and caught at the long, black gown of the old priest! The fire was spreading fast to every part of the room!

In the light of the fire, I recognized the young woman who was still sleeping under the effect of a wonderful dream! I felt an unexpected bomb-blast below my abdomen! She had the profile of my own dear wife!

Outside the hut, I heard a cracking sound; it was the breaking of the topmost branch of the jack-fruit tree. The shrieks and shouts of the Fire Force employees and of the youngsters who drew unemployment allowance resounded in the atmosphere.

The old priest, whose whole body was burning with fire, ran here and there in the hut, seeking a way to go out. From his body fire spread to every part of the hut and I saw flames licking up the long, red gown of the evangelist's wife too! She, with an ear-breaking shriek, took the boy from the bed and ran out of the hut, into the courtyard and, then, into the street.

Realizing the fact that the hut and the old priest had become one and the same, I ran out following the evangelist's wife in order to save the boy from her burning body. In her efforts to put out the flames on her body, she threw the child towards me and stood for a moment staring at the broken branch of the jack-fruit tree! The employees of the Fire Force had already taken her husband's body to the government hospital for post mortem!

For a moment, she stood by the middle of the street like a pillar of fire and, then, ran towards her fire-ball of a hut! There the young, beautiful woman might still be sleeping on the white carpet, completely immersed in some sweet dream!

I looked at the face of the boy who was thrown to my hands by the evangelist's wife. Again, I felt a bomb-blast below my abdomen! He was my own child, born from my own blood and marrow!

The neighboring hut was completely burned down in the fire! My son was peacefully sleeping in my numbed hands. The alarm-bell of the fire-engine echoed in my ears like an everlasting knell. I looked around to see whether there was any

other jack-fruit tree with a heaven-touching branch on it!
And the evening and the morning were the fourth day!

Author's Notes: Man is a rational animal but the spirit of evangelism dormant in every religion makes many believers crazy, eccentric and even abnormal. His blind faith will lead him to a fool's paradise, transforming him into a fake enthusiast, a pseudo-idealist and, finally, an anti-social terrorist who digs his own grave of eternal damnation. A true believer in God must keep an equal but safe distance away from both religious superstition and rationalism.

PART TWO

Selected from Stories Written

11. The Sobbing Guitar
12. Incarnations
13. Through the Fog
14. The Roof-Frame
15. The Star-Night
16. Face to Face with a Novelist
17. The Vendor Tooth Powder
18. The Dowry-Tragedy and a Few Old Sayings
19. A Simple Cure for Pimples
20. Where Ignorance is Bliss
21. Who Should Cast the First Stone?

11

THE SOBBING GUITAR

"**Ay,** Mister! Life is to enjoy! Drink life to the lees!" Lobo said as he took the glass in his hands, and poured the rest of the liquor into his mouth.

"But…! At any case, one thing is very clear! The moral side of your community is very weak!" Someone said in a low voice.

Those words irritated Lobo. He struck his fists angrily on the table and cried: "What man? Think, morality is just a matter of opportunity!"

"Very correct!" Most of them supported him, showing thumbs inward.

"Drink some more, my dear friend!" Lobo said as he patted on my back.

I raised my head and said: "Excuse me, Mr. Lobo. Usually I don't drink liquor. But….! Now I took it only because you compelled me so much."

Lobo laughed aloud and said: "Good boy! See, behavior is just a matter of circumstances! Do you understand?"

"One-hundred percent correct!" Most of them cried aloud, raising their hands in his support.

It was late in the night when the party was over. Most of them, including Lobo, were in a drunken mood! So, I took up the duty of taking Lobo home, for I had drunk only a bit for the 'company's sake'.

It was a hard job to take Lobo to his house. He put his left hand around my neck, resting most of the weight of his body on my right shoulder, and staggered all the way. All along the road, he continued his chattering and, then at times, turned to sobbing and crying. He became very talkative when we reached the street where most of the members of his community lived.

He said: "Friend! Didn't you hear what they said about our community? Didn't they say that we have no moral sense? We accept it fully. We have got no belief in morality, because we are sinners. Our grandpas and grandmas had no morality. If they had it, how could they produce a breed like us, in the soil of India? Our mere nativity is in sin. As long as our skin is white, we have no escape from this sin."

He again started sobbing. Refrains of heavenly songs flowed from every house on the street. A magic world of guitar, violin and piano! I said to myself: Ha! If I were born as an Anglo-Indian, I could have enjoyed life like a bottle of wine....!

From most of the houses, we heard the rising wild tunes of cabaret dances. The thought of the red beauties who were shaking their bodies according to those tunes bubbled in my mind. The tinkling sounds of glasses, plates, knives and forks as well as the cries of cheers resounded in the atmosphere. A flood of laughter! The ebb and flow of passions! And then....! Lobo walked slowly and silently.

When we were walking up the steps of his house, I heard someone playing a tragic tune on a guitar. Lobo whispered in my ears: "That's my sister, Dolly."

"Dolly! Open the door, please!" Lobo said aloud, knocking at the door, through which the guitar music escaped.

The sound of the guitar stopped. The door opened wide.

Lobo entered the room, clutching to my shoulder. His nose, cheeks and eyes were reddened because of heavy intoxication. Dolly was surprised for a moment, seeing me, a stranger before her.

I said calmly: "Excuse me! Today it seems Lobo drank a bit too much."

"What? Too much? What do you mean by that?" Lobo stared at me.

"Oh! Now he's alright!" I said just to change the subject.

After winking at me, Lobo turned towards his sister, and said: "Dolly! Meet my friend, an artist, a writer and a bachelor!" He laughed voluptuously.

"Glad to meet you!" She said with a smile and extended her hand. The lack of experience on my part in shaking hands with girls, forced me to raise my hands together to greet her in the Indian fashion. She looked at me in surprise and said sweetly: "Please, take a seat!"

Mr. Lobo held on to my shoulders and forced me to sit on the sofa.

Dolly, with a perpetual smile on her face, looked at me and asked: "What would you prefer to drink?"

Lobo stared at her angrily and howled: "What a question? Bring some hot ones....!"

I said gently: "I'll be very happy if you give me some cold water....!"

"Of course! Please, wait a few minutes!" She said and hurried towards the next room where the refrigerator was placed, in order to fetch cold water for me.

Lobo turned towards me and murmured in my ears: "Poor girl! Behaves like a mere country lass! She doesn't like our social customs and manners. For many weeks, I have tried my best to tame her. I am giving her many chances to move freely among my friends, I mean, friends like you! Oh, it's alright!

Sooner or later, everything will be changed."

I reluctantly raised my doubt to Mr. Lobo: "Then....! One day, suppose....you understand.....that your sister is rape-pregnant....I mean, out of wedlock!"

Lobo laughed aloud and said in a confidential tone: "That problem will not arise! Our girls take special precautions, I mean, a certain kind of tablet, regularly. Or...supposing they become pregnant, so what? There are so many methods of escaping from that pit too!"

Dolly entered the room with a glass of cold water. I looked at that young girl. Instead of returning my curious look, she made an innocent smile. Her stature and figure exceeded her age. She was wearing a silk nightgown embroidered with a beautiful picture in the arabesque style. The back and front sides of its neck was fairly and attractively cut to the shoulder level.

Seeing that I was drinking just cold water, Lobo grinned and said: "Bloody fool! Just a moment.....! Excuse me!"

He stood up suddenly and said, as he remembered some extraordinary matter: "Dolly, he is my intimate friend! Treat him well!"

He swung sideways and walked towards his room. He closed its doors with a bang, and I heard him falling down on his bed with a thud!

Unknowingly, I shuddered myself at his words: 'Treat him well!' Those words echoed and re-echoed in my ears. The meaning of those words was too clear to an Anglo-Indian girl. I looked up at Dolly's face. It was pale as if there was not a drop of blood on her face. She looked downcast with an air of sadness and did not dare to even look at me.

I stood up from the chair and said to Dolly: "See you later, Dolly! Thank you very much!"

Moving towards the door, I murmured: "Goodnight!"

To her my behavior was new or rather strange, in the short span of her life!

"Really!" She muttered with stark surprise and stared at me as if she had heard some unbelievable news. Then, she gently asked: "Didn't you hear what my brother said?"

"Yah, I heard! But I'm not an Anglo-Indian!" Turning my face towards the door, I said once again: "So....Goodnight!"

"Please, wait a moment!" She blocked my way and said: "Tomorrow is my birthday and by eight in the evening, there'll be a party. I wish you too should be here!"

"Well! I'll try....!" Once again I turned to walk, but she immediately caught my hand and said: "Please, wish me goodnight in our own fashion!"

I was puzzled and looked foolishly, thinking for a moment what to do! She put her hands over my neck and pressed her lips on my cheeks and said repeatedly: "Wish me goodnight! Wish me goodnight!"

I gently kissed her forehead and whispered: "Goodnight, darling! Goodnight and sweet dreams!"

Slowly I walked down the steps and entered the street. Even then, there waved the streaming music of guitar, violin and piano in the atmosphere. And...the sound of tired footsteps of intoxicated dancers!

I reached my room after a few minutes' walk. I still felt the warmth of Dolly's kiss on my cheeks. Unknowingly my palm crept towards my cheek, caressed it for a second and, then, I placed my lips heavily on my palm, where I also felt the warmth of her lips.

Next morning, Lobo came and patted me on my back and said: "Brave boy! I think that yesterday you must have very well enjoyed Dolly's company, eh? She asked me to invite you as a distinguished guest for today's birthday party. Congratulations! A rare luck, and for you only!"

I felt the bad sense of his words. For a moment I searched for a few apt words to answer him. But he waved his hand and slowly walked away, saying: "So....Bye! Bye! See you in the evening!"

That evening, I reached Lobo's house, with a sort of fear, thinking whether I could participate full-heartedly, a party where mostly Anglo-Indians were present.

Dolly ran towards me and greeted me with that perpetual smile present on her face. She led me into the main hall and offered a seat. Yet I found in her bluish eyes the wavelets of some stagnant sorrow which was unknown to me. By eight o'clock sharp, the room was filled with guests. Mr. Lobo had already arranged everything for the feast – drinks, snacks, other food-items and also dancing.

The guests crowded around the table where the birthday cake was placed. Dolly blew out eighteen candles and together all of us sang: Happy Birthday to you....!

When we were clapping our hands, Lobo took a piece of cake and pushed it into Dolly's mouth! She also returned a piece to him.

Heavenly music, with enchanting rhythm and tone, floated around us, as the tape recorder began to rotate. Our tables were filled with non-vegetarian dishes, liquor and carbonated drinks.

Many of the guests suggested the name of Dolly as the 'Queen of the Night' and she was elected. I clapped my hands heartily when she received the crown of the queen of the night! Dolly! She was a real queen at that time!

Soon, the tape recorder played the songs for slow-motion dance and both young and old couples moved around the hall hand in hand. Gradually, the music as well as the dancing doubled its speed.

I drew my chair to a corner and sat there carelessly watching the dancers, for I did not know their western dancing.

Suddenly, a faint sound of sobbing and crying reached my ears. On the verandah, Dolly was speaking with a gentleman who was not familiar to me. I heard her speaking, sometimes angrily, sometimes with an air of authority and other times pleading in the midst of their conversation. That unknown man's cold and rough words melted in the high sounds and laughter which rose from the main hall. Minutes passed and I heard heavy sounds of boots stepping down to the street.

Dolly entered the room and I looked keenly at her rosy cheeks. Two or three drops of tears hung on her chin and they shone brightly like pearls in the mercury light of the dancing hall. After a moment, she saw me. Soon, she cupped her mouth in order to gulp down an out-bursting cry. She ran into the inner room. I sat down on my chair, staring at those dancing images which moved like ghosts!

When the first dancing session was over, Dolly came into the room with a guitar in her hands. With great interest, I watched her long white fingers stroking the strings of her guitar. She started her music with a couplet of that tragic song which I had heard her playing on the previous night. But soon she began to play a wild tune. She played so wildly that I feared her soft fingers would be injured. She continued her playing until what I expected, happened. When the guests clapped their hands with cheers, she threw off her guitar like a mad woman. They were all puzzled and looked agape, while she poured a full glass of liquor and drank, without adding even a single drop of water!

Lobo clapped his hands and said aloud with a laugh: "Sabhash! Sabhash! Well done, darling! Only now you are a real girl!"

Dolly came to my side with two glasses and a bottle of whisky. She immediately filled both glasses. Magi, the voluptuous beauty among the group, began her cabaret dance.

Dolly compelled me much to take a few more drinks.

The 'golden eagle' which was trying to fly up looked fiercely at me! Forgetting everything, Dolly forced me again and again to drink. The cruelty or revenge that shone in her eyes frightened me. Her cheeks, stained by dried tears, seemed pale and white like the face of a corpse.

While all the guests were immersed in the cabaret of the golden goddess Magi, Dolly put both her hands around my neck and kissed me four or five times, wildly on my lips and, then, said with a shivering voice: "Wish me goodnight, my dear late comer, wish me goodnight, my dearest too late comer, wish me everlasting goodnight....!"

I said nothing and sat there like a wooden statue. Her lips were as cold as an ice-cube. Without waiting for my reply, Dolly ran away into her room. Sometime later, I bade farewell to Mr. Lobo and stepped down to the street and went to my room.

I was too tired after the night's heavy drinking and I slept very late in the morning. Some of my friends called aloud and forcefully woke me up and said: "Here's tragic news for you! Last night, our Lobo's sister took sleeping pills and committed suicide!"

A shiver ran through me, from head to foot, and, like a hysterical patient, I cried: "What? Is it true?"

Someone commented: "Poor girl! She was betrayed! The doctor said that she had six months' pregnancy! And that bastard has wife and children in the neighboring town!"

Still on many evenings, inside my head, someone strokes the strings of a guitar, the painful tunes of a tragic song!

Author's notes: Many communities in India, irrespective of their religious beliefs, face social problems, sometimes, a sort of identity crisis, in the pull and push of the eastern and western cultures; and the case of the Anglo-Indian community is typical. Years ago, Golden Eagle was a brand of top-quality whisky in India. Though many changes have occurred to my selection and treatment of subjects in short stories, the Sobbing Guitar is really my pet-story, as it is my first published English story, in the Employment Bulletin (1977), Gangtok, Sikkim.

12

INCARNATIONS

I was at the end of my tether. I opened the packet and counted the sleeping pills in it. There were twenty five tablets. Corresponding to my age! Each tablet for each year!

Yes! It was time to end my too long journey. Twenty five years were very, very long to me though I forgot to live. Nobody was here to mourn over my death. Perhaps, Fanny might shed a few drops of tears. But Time the Healer would bring consolation to her and she too would forget this unwanted element.

I looked at the glass, full of sweet milk, brought by my loving friend Fanny in whose house I had been staying. I put the sleeping pills, one by one, into the glass and stirred it. Then, I waited for the heaven-sent moment to drink it.

It needed a moment's super courage to commit suicide. Many a time, I had tried to commit suicide but, alas, I was not a brave man. Without getting some peace of mind how could one commit suicide? Whenever I tried to do this heavenly act, an immediate distraction would occur before me like an ill-omen!

I liked to commit suicide in a lovely way. To die in the midst of sleep is the happiest thing one could expect in human life. So many times, Yama, the God of Death, appeared before me in the form of sleeping tablets. But he was always reluctant to welcome this unfortunate creature to his dark world. It was a tragedy with me that whenever I decided to do a brave act, an immediate impediment would rise before me like a fence of barbed wire!

On the previous day, Fanny said to me: "Oh, Mr. King! You're a fool!"

Yes! I admitted it. It was not my fault that I was born on the first of April. And April was the best month, according to Chaucer! I was a born fool! I wanted to live like a fool and I wished to die like a fool. I knew that a fool's coxcomb was much greater than a king's crown!

Fanny struck her beautiful right palm on her forehead and cried: "Oh, my goodness! Who gave you the name King? It ought to be 'Beggar'!"

Yes! I admitted it too. I was a beggar and I knocked at each and every door to get a job. All of them turned me out. Some of them sympathized with me; others advised me to start a small-scale industry. Some others laughed at me and asked me to join politics and a few others even threatened me. Wasn't I a beggar?

I looked at the latest letter sent by my mother. She wrote: "Believe in God, my son. He will help you!"

Yes! I admitted it. Many a time God appeared before me in the form of a cup of tea or a piece of bread or in the form of an interview card. On a hot summer day, when I was wandering through the streets of Hyderabad in search of a job, God appeared before me in the form of a cup of tea. Again, when I was a hungry, ticket-less traveler on a train, He appeared before me somewhere in Maharashtra, in the form of a packet of rice. And what about those bundles of interview cards which were sacredly kept in my file? They were pages from the Bible for me! They helped me, at least, to prolong my life a bit more!

Once my father said: "It's the fault with your horoscope,

my child. You have to suffer all these misfortunes up to the age of thirty-five. Then the stars will shower blessings on you!"

I could not admit it, however! Aries was not a bad star. I knew only one thing, the Goddess of Ill-luck. I had had a lot more experience with her than any other gods or goddesses. Like Janus, the Greek goddess, she had two faces, as I experienced, one a beautiful and the other an ugly one. She, sometimes, looked at me with her smiling face. But at the nick of an opportunity, she would turn her face away from me, after giving me a glimpse of hope. Then, I attended my interview as a rejuvenated man. But when the result came out, to my utter distress, my Goddess would show her ugly face. She continued this 'hide and seek' game for a number of years.

How long could one hang on to the threads of misfortune? All these years, my imagination cheated me much. My hopes burned me into ashes. I should have nipped them in their buds. Many a time, I had fancied that I would become the king of India or even the emperor of the world! I had imagined that I could solve all the problems of this world with a magical snap of my fingers. But, alas, I was a fool, a born fool!

This world is not for fools; neither for lovers and poets nor for mad men. I knew it and, as I was a born fool, I had no other choice. I took the glass in my hand, collected a bit of courage, and brought it to my lips to drink the potion.

Oh, my Goddess Ill-luck! A knock came on my door and I looked up cursing myself. Fanny rushed into my room with an excited face. She cried in ecstasy: "Oh, King! How lucky you are! See, this interview card!"

She pushed an interview card into my hands. Another incarnation of God! The beautiful face of my Goddess Ill-luck!

I said to her with a grave face: "Just keep it in your hands. Tomorrow you may put it in my coffin!"

She stared at me. Then, she noticed the glass filled with

sweet milk and the empty cover of sleeping pills lying on my table.

"Oh, you fool! How dare you?" She shrieked and then threw the glass of milk through the window. A moment's silence, and then, she hid her face in her palms and sobbed bitterly.

I kept quiet, thinking about the unlucky man who turned back after touching the plough. God once again appeared before me in the form of an interview card so that I had to attend yet another interview.

Was it to prolong my life a bit more? Was it only to know that I was rejected by the interview board? Was it to prepare another sweet potion? I did not know....!

Author's notes: Wait! My dear unemployed youngsters, wait! One day, you too will get a chance, as it happened in my life. He who tore open your mouth will provide food for it! In fact, I wrote this as a part of my novel, *Upon This Bank and Shoal,* but had to change it into a short story for a magazine; and Fanny remains as one of my favorite characters.

13

THROUGH THE FOG

The fog…..! The thick fog…..!

(It's very difficult to see even the persons who are standing nearby! Then….what about those who stand far away…?)

All…..all were shadows……mere shadows……!

(This is the world! This is man! And this is human relationship!!)

Oh, fog…….thickest fog……..!

(Am I becoming a philosopher, when moving step by step towards my unknown destination or destiny, searching the rare gaps in this thick fog?)

The fog…..or the mist…….!

(It arises slowly from the valley and, then, spreads all over the world…..like some eternal sorrow!)

Oh, this thick fog……!

(It makes me older. The heat in my body turns into steam and jumps out through my mouth and nose. Blood thickens in my veins. I sense the smell of death on my clothes. Each moment, my clothes tighten on my body, strangling me. What? Is my way going to an end? Going to an end……?)

Through the fog came an eerie song…..!

(It may be rising from the military barracks situated up on the mountain tops. Can the fog prevent a song, when someone is singing with a full-throated ease?)

If these verses had not rung in my ears, years ago my journey would have come to an end….!

(Dearest song, penetrate into my ears….strike on the rusted strings of my brain and raise in my heart, at least, a tiny note of consolation! Thus…..thus, let the length of my path, a path with un-climbable heights on one side and the un-descendible depths on the other, be further extended.)

Many years ago, when I had played truant from my own home and was standing on the muddy floor of a vegetable shop situated near some second mile-stone, trying to quench my hunger with a stolen carrot, I saw the fog, first in my life, rising from the darkness of a culvert. Then too, this eerie song came towards me through the fog, in the form of a distant relative. While this innocent child was walking on that strange land, through the fog, with a distant, drunken relative, to an unknown destination, I heard him saying: "Boy, its mist…..! Ah, the mist!"

(Now, the fog is mixed with a disgusting smell, rising from some pigsty. Being disturbed by the fog, the pigs are purring and squeaking…!)

'Oy, dhaju! Kata?'

(Oh, brother! Where are you going? Who is asking? My mind? Or this shadow of a person that comes nearer and closer?)

Snow began to fall. The approaching shadow turned into a beautiful girl, covered in a woolen blanket.

(The fog…..! Is it turning into smog….?)

"Aaja ekdum jado chhai!" She whispered to herself.

(It is too cold today. Hmm….! Only today? Every day it is cold, tree-trembling cold!)

Shaking away the powder-snow from her woolen blanket, she said, "Yasto kuiro ma timi kasari janchhau?"

(How can you go through this fog? How can I? When life

71

itself is drowned in the fog, how cannot one help going? No….! Where to go? Into the thickest fog….?)

She continued with a smile, "Aaja timi mere ghar aau ani aago tapera jaau."

(You come to my house and warm yourself! Now….! Here one gets an aim for the journey. There is a glimpse of hope even in the thickest fog! Why shouldn't I go to her house and warm up my body?)

With the shadow of the beautiful girl, I crawled into a hut, filled with the damp smell of pig-dung. A hut with an old man who was sitting on the floor and putting dried twigs into the coal-heater. He did not even care for the newcomers!

(The old man…..! Hmm….! A man who puts dried twigs into the fire…..! Well! What else can he do?)

She rocked the back of the old man and I heard her asking, "Bapu, aaja tapai ghumaa janu hunna?"

(Father, aren't you going outside for a walk? Hmm….! Father….! Father….?)

The old man raised his tired eyes at her. Tears were hanging on the lids of his small eyes.

(Is it because of the smoke rising from the coal-heater? Or because of the fog…the thick fog….?)

"Kina runu bhako?" She stared at him.

(Why are you crying? Why…..? Why….!)

"Teysai….." the old man murmured.

(Simply….simply crying….? Just simply….!)

She poured rakshi, a local drink, into a glass and gave it to him. The old man drank it, even without adding a single drop of water. Then….he took a burning twig from the coal-heater and lit his hookah which was filled with tobacco. He went out of the hut, stooping, and walked into the fog…..into the thickest fog……!

(Behind the hut, the pigs are squeaking…..! An omen? A

good one....? Or a bad one....?)

She took the woolen blanket off her shoulder, shook it twice, spread it over the sack-cote and said, "Aunosh, palank ma basnosh."

(Come on.....! Do sit on this cote...!)

When I sat on the creaking cote and caressed my unshaven face, she pushed the coal-heater nearer to the side of the cote.

(Fuming twigs in the coal-heater....! The twigs dropped by the old man....! By the old generation...?)

She poured some rakshi into an ugly glass and asked, "Tapai alikati rakshi khanu hunchha?"

(Do you take liquor? Hmm....! Well....! Well....?)

I stared at the ash-covering embers of the coal-heater and murmured hesitatingly, "Machanga paisa chhaina....!"

(I have no money with me. No money....? Money....! No!)

The hands which carried the rakshi-bottle and the ugly glass trembled. For a moment, she stared at me, and then....into the fog that was blowing into the hut.....into the dilapidated hut.

(Is it fog......? Or smog.....? What a cold it is! How cold am I....? Or she...?)

She mixed a little water in the rakshi and came towards me. I took the glass from her hand, looking at the fog that was gushing into the hut. She sat near me on the cote and stretched her hands over the coal-heater, and warmed them. With a deep sigh, she said, "Aajkal koishang paisa chhaina!"

(There's no money in anybody's hand, now-a-days! Poor girl! Do you think that there is no money in anybody's hands only because those people like me who come into this hut have no money with them? There is money in everybody's hands. But there is no money in your hands and in mine!)

Somebody's voice of alarm or embarrassment came into the hut through the fog. She was startled and stood there like a statue. Then....! She looked into the thickest fog through the tin-door of the hut. A few shadows came into the hut carrying something....!

Oh, no! The blood-covered body of the old man....! Among his paralyzed fingers, there was the cold hookah; its fire had already extinguished! The hookah, filled with strong tobacco...!

(Where is the eerie song? Can the fog prevent it? Oh, prevent it....?)

When the girl cried aloud, embracing the motionless body of the old man, I heard a shadow speaking through the fog, "Tulo khola ma budo manchhe ladyo..."

(The old man has fallen into a deep pit. Well.....! His way is ended and his journey is over!)

Ash filled up in the coal-heater. Somebody pulled out the hookah from the cold fingers of the old man and placed it on the cote.

(No eerie song can come through the thickest fog......!)

I blew off the ash and took an ember from the coal-heater and lit the half-burned tobacco in the hookah of the old man. At a stretch, I gulped the whole rakshi from the glass, and then, taking the hookah, went out of the hut and walked into the fog....into the all enveloping thickest fog......

Author's notes: The dialogue is in the Nepali language. Dear readers of non-native English please change those twelve sentences into your mother tongue and feel homely.

I changed them into Amharic language and published it in *The Voice of Ethiopia (2008),* together with other pieces of writings in English from Ethiopia.

14

THE ROOF-FRAME

As if somebody is striking in the brain with a wooden hammer....! As if somebody is driving a chisel into the innermost part of the heart....a chisel made red-hot in the fire of the bellows and seasoned its edge by dipping in cold water....a chisel sharpened by filing against the sharpening-plank smeared with white-stone powder.....!

The nauseating smell of medicines and lotions penetrates through the nostrils and touches the soft strings of the lungs to produce an unclear sound.....! The whole body slips into a sort of complete paralysis.....! The mind tries to say numerous things and the body denies moving even a bit......!

From the bottle that hangs from the stand, upside down like human life, life-giving glucose water flows drop by drop through the rubber tube.....through the glass-pipe....into the vein.....into the heart.....into the broken heart.....!

Is it true that we all see the whole of our past life, as if in a flashback, just before our death....? Is it not the cry of a new born babe that I hear from a far distance....? Is it the beginning of that flashback....? Is this that horrible moment to leave everything and everybody to the hands of posterity....? Is it that inevitable moment in which every living creature faces utter helplessness....? The final encounter with fate....?

The cry of the new born babe....! Somebody should have

cut the natal cord and, thereby, my connection with my mother....! From here onwards I am alone....alone to face the tragic realities of life....! I lose the warmth of the womb of my mother....and I lose the security of the natal cord.....forever! I have nothing but my sole entity.....! I must live till my death....all, all alone!

And now is the initiation ceremony.....! After a jerking in the flashback.....!

On that day of the initiation......early morning.....mother poured a handful of coconut oil on the very top-centre of the head.....to cool the head, they say! Someone guided towards the temple-pond to have a bath in the cold water......into a pond full of lotus-flowers, white water lilies and green water-weeds and moss!

Walked towards the house, wearing the wet loin-cloth....! Then smearing the forehead with holy ash and sandal paste.....! Someone forced me to squat on the mat made of dried screw pine-leaves, spread in front of the house......in the courtyard where a square area was consecrated for the boy who had to become a good carpenter in future....!

The concentration was only on the family goddess.....! Smoke spiraled from the lighted incense-sticks.....light spread from the burning cloth-stics in the ghee-lamp....raw rice...... boiled rice......dried rice.....flowers....basil leaves......pop rice.....red sugar candy......rice flakes......bananas.......dried grapes.....! Everything kept in small piles sacredly on a fresh banana leaf.....by the tip of the banana leaf......!

Then began the formal rites and ceremonies......of prayers and chants.....and, finally, somebody gave the holy offerings to eat.....!

Now, it's the turn of the father......! Father came, chewing the betel leaf with areca-nut, lime and tobacco....a full mouth.....and after a long spit of the blood-colored betel juice towards the outer part of the courtyard.....to the farthest spot, with harsh gurgling sound.....! Then, sitting by my side, drew lines on the sugar-sand of the courtyard, with the tip of the wooden hammer's handle....and taught for the first time how to fix the complicated roof-frame of a house....!

Three times he did the same thing.....every time erasing the lines off the sand with his palm.....and finally, asking me to draw them from my memory.....! As the lines were correctly drawn, tears of happiness flowed down the unshaven cheeks of father....falling at the very top of my head....!

Placing his hand on my head and caressing my curly hair, he blessed: "Velu, my son! You'll become better than all other carpenters.....! Be thou blessed by our family goddess and by our Vishwakarma, the deity of carpenters......and by Perumthachchan, the Great Carpenter, our ancestor.....!"

Flashback continues......though most of it is vague.....! Oh! If only all of them turn clear....!

Yes! And again.....on another day.....!

Selecting certain thrown-out wooden planks and pieces of wood.....cutting and smoothening them with a chisel..... drawing angles and squares on them with a pencil....cutting notches, grooves and clefts on them....a roof-frame was made for the palm-parrot's cage.....!

Seeing its technical perfection, father gave kisses on the forehead, with his hot lips reddened with betel juice....!

And what happened to that cage of the singing palm-parrot? It swings still in the wind....hanging on a wire, tied to the projected plank of the roof...at the tip of the plank that extended towards the verandah.....without any change..... without any damage.....!

And what happened to that singing palm-parrot? Years passed since the black cat had caught and killed it.....! And they said that birds would not live long in that cage.....!

And what about that father who showered kisses on the forehead? Father who came to the house in the evenings with tired legs, incapable of walking, after drinking too much from the toddy shop....father who gave kisses that smelt betel leaf and alcohol.....? He was only a father first....then a grandfather.....and then, withdrew himself towards the back of the stage.....behind the curtain.....into the depth of oblivion... into the lap of earth.....under a heap of soil.....under the piled up pebbles and white-stones...forever...forever and a day.....!

The vision is not bright.....; it's so dim and it fades so fast.....so fast that it fails to stand on the screen.....the screen of the mind.....; it vanishes before its recognition....so fast like the flash of a lightning.....!

"Velu! You'll have a boon today! The Zamindar has sent me to tell you to come to his house. You'll have a real harvest!" The manager of the Zamindar appeared to be very happy.

Before starting to the Zamindar's house.....stood in front of the family deity for a moment in deep meditation.....also concentrating on Lord Krishna.....on Vishwakarma.....on Perumthachchan, the great carpenter of carpenters.....on all the souls of the dead ancestors for whom annual rites and ceremonies were performed on time.... For whom alcoholic drinks were offered every year.....!

Then.....the mind was full of hopes.....full of consoling dreams.....full of wishes that cooled the heart......!

It's all cool here.....cold creeps up from the feet.....towards the heart.....!

"Carpenter! We want a new house!" The Zamindar said without much beating around the bush.

The words of the Zamindar echoed the warning given by the father. If the client says, "I want a house," don't build it but if he says, "We want a house," build it. See, a house is built not merely for human beings alone, but it's a shelter for animals, birds and even insects.....!

"Of course! Let's begin the work on the very next auspicious day, Sir!"

"Oh, that's great!" The Zamindar's son who was learning to become a doctor said in excitement. He continued, "Respected Carpenter! I've to go back to the medical college only after seeing the roof-frame fixed on the top! Understand?"

Understand....? Nothing is clear....; it's all beyond the understanding of ordinary minds.....!

On the very next auspicious day, by the most suitable moment of the day...., when the sharpened chisel entered into the rose-wood plank.....a wooden plank with the color of the clotted blood..., the carpenter's heart was beating fast.....! When at the force of the wooden hammer, the first piece of chiseled wood......separated from the mother-plank....flew up in the air.....rolling and whirling in the air......and fell down upside down on the ground......, the carpenter was shocked...! He stared into that lifeless piece of wood and he immersed into some deep thought for a moment....! A heavy sob rose up from the innermost part of the heart.....! The traditional science of the carpenter won't go wrong.....! Everything is as clear as daylight......! With a trembling voice, the query came out from the heart of hearts, "Master! Is there any pregnant woman in the family?"

"Oh, no! Nobody's pregnant, Carpenter!" The Zamindar said with a laugh.

Well! The science of intuition won't lie! Again, enquired with some fear, "Is there any carrying cow or other domestic animals?"

"Oh, none! Well! What's the matter, Carpenter?" asked the Zamindar.

"Oh, nothing! Nothing, master!" Once again the chisel pierced the rose-wood. There was grief and pain evident in the voice, "I was planning to arrange the marriage of my daughter Malti, and send her to her husband's home....!"

"So what, Carpenter?" asked the Zamindar's son who was studying in a foreign country. Wasn't there some anxiety in his words? Or was it mere compassion for a poor man's family....?

"Oh, it's alright! Everything happens according to the will of God!" There was a tone of self-consolation. Words came out with much effort, "It's ominous to have pregnant creatures in our families till the new house is completed!" A tone of fear and warning echoed in those words.....!

"Oh, nonsense!" said aloud the young master who belonged to the new generation. A deep sigh of utter helplessness and despair came up from the depth of a carpenter's heart!

Scenes come and go...; sometimes the images are clear, other times quite vague.....! The focus is improper......!

On the auspicious day of placing the first big wooden beam on the top of the wall as a base for the roof-frame.....! Dried rice and rice flakes, sugar candy and banana pieces.......were all placed on the tip-half of a banana leaf.....! Dried, husked coconut, split into two equal halves with a chisel.....placed reverently on the banana leaf, like two bowls.....! Water and coconut water mixed, in equal portions, and poured into those coconut bowls......! Into which the holy basil leaf was put, after meditating on the holy deity for a few minutes.......and then.....stared at the movement of the basil leaf in the coconut water.....in the coconut bowls......!

After floating and moving fast here and there for a few seconds, the leaf stopped at a corner of the coconut bowl......! The carpenter watched its position and calculated its connotations in the zodiac and in the position of the constellations.....and immersed in deep thought......! When the divine figure of Lord Ayyappa appeared in the mind, the carpenter offered himself to go for the holy pilgrimage to

Sabarimala: Oh, the Holy Feet of the benign deity! I shall climb up the Holy Eighteen Steps for the next festival.....! Please save us from all misfortunes.....!

And then, on another auspicious day.....of raising the wooden roof-frame up on the walls of the house.....over the four wooden beams joined properly at all the four corners of the house.....the day of drinking and merry making for all the workers, masons and carpenters.....!

After offering new clothes to all laborers who helped in the construction of the house.....the Zamindar said, "Today my son is going abroad to continue his medical studies! He'll return only after three years...!"

While walking down the steps of the Zamindar's house, the young master came and told him to come to a lonely spot.....! He gave the carpenter an additional packet of new clothes and said, "Give this to your daughter Malti. She has no one else to give such things....!"

How kind of him.....! Heart was overflowing with love and respect......! When the young master left, the carpenter's heart wished him all the best....; his lips were chanting, "Lord Krishna! Give luck to my young master!"

"Malti! My daughter! Come and see this packet! Our young master gave this to you!" The carpenter's face glowed with pride!

The daughter took the new clothes and pressed it to her heart. The carpenter continued with an air of satisfaction, "The young master has gone for higher studies. He'll come back only after two or three years....!"

The packet of clothes slipped down from her hands and fell down on the muddy floor.....the floor blackened with cow-dung and charcoal.....! The carpenter stood in a stupor! The daughter ran into the inner room with a loud cry.....! Through her sobs, came out the words, "Three years......! Oh, God!

Three years....! He promised me wedding clothes and he gave it.......but not the wedding ring and the garland......!"

On the steel stand, the bottle of glucose-water was hanging upside down......the medicated water flows drop by drop.....like drops of tears.....hot, blistering tears......!

Again....the flashback...just like caricatures of shadows...!

The next day early morning, Malti came with a cup of steaming black coffee. While taking the cup from her hands, the carpenter's hands trembled.....! Raising the cup of hot coffee to the lips, he looked into the wet eyes of his daughter.....then, on her swollen belly.....! The cup and the coffee fell down from his hands.....also a few drops of hot tears.....!

Taking the chisel and the wooden hammer, he walked towards the Zamindar's house. Throughout the way, he was murmuring, "It's fate, my dear daughter! It's all our fate, my dear child...!"

Climbing up to the top-most beam of the roof-frame, the carpenter carved the holy sign 'OM' on the corner plank. As he finished the work, Gopi the neighbor-boy came, running and crying, "Oh, come and help! Sister Malti has fallen into the well and died....!"

Darkness strained into the eyes! The sharpened chisel unknowingly slipped away from the hand.....rolling and whirling.....it came down and pierced the raw-floor....! He felt dizziness; darkness crept into his eyes, and his body rolled down to the ground.....! From his paralyzed hand....the wooden hammer slipped away.....and it fell.....hitting here and there.....on the planks of the roof-frame......and finally, down at the courtyard......!

"My master! While I fixed the roof-frame of your house, it was the roof-frame of my house that fell down! The whole roof of my family has fallen down forever, my master!" The carpenter wished to cry aloud. But he felt as if his words were tangled somewhere in his throat.....as if his tongue was paralyzed......!

Gopi, the neighbor-boy, was talking to someone, "Poor old carpenter! His beautiful parrot-cage also fell down......! It was hanging from the corner plank of his house on a rusted wire......! They say that parrots won't survive in that cage....!"

The carpenter felt as if the sharp teeth and nails of the black cat that had caught and eaten the palm-parrot entered into his heart.....! He heard the helpless fluttering and the wing-beating of the parrot....also its frightened cries....! Was it really the voice of the palm-parrot.....or.....or of his daughter Malti......?

"Alas! My daughter...!"

Then all......all came to a standstill......the thumping of the heart.....the movement of the eyes......and even the dripping of the glucose through the glass-tube into the vein.....into the lifeless vein!

Author's notes: This story is dedicated to the memory of that ninety-year-old grandma who I met at Palace Hospital, Aleppey, Kerala, where my mother was recovering after a major operation, during the summer holidays of 1971. She was there to look after her grandson who had been admitted there following an accident, and with stories from her life, she kept me awake during those critical nights. She belonged to the Vishwakarma or carpenter-smith caste, and I still remember her face with deep furrows of wrinkles, her toothless smiles, the corners of her 'mouth touching the ears' and the lobs of 'ears touching the shoulders'!

15

THE STAR-NIGHT

The child was in great excitement. He said in a joyful tone, "Grandpa, today there's the star-night!"

"Star-night?" The old man hesitated for a moment. He nodded his head with some understanding and said, "Good, at least this damn rainy season should come to an end!" Heaving a long sigh, he continued, "I can see everything with my mind's eye! The clear blue sky! Just like a canopy of blue canvas with a sort of mirror-work! An illumination of the first order, isn't it, my child?"

"This grandpa doesn't know even a thing!" The child said in a regretful tone. He continued, "Everybody says star-night, star-night! Brother Appu also said the same thing! But I don't know its meaning, Grandpa!" The child felt sadness and despair...!

"Don't worry, my child!" The old man consoled the child. He said, "Come, dear! Let's go to that place from where the music comes. If we have a few coins, it'll be great comfort in these rainy days!" The old man's voice was full of confidence and determination.

"That's what I said, grandpa! Today's the star-night! All the film actors and actresses are coming here! They'll be given prizes!" The boy once again became enthusiastic.

"Oh, really! Then, I must've heard about such meetings!"

The old man thought for a while. With a heavy breath, he whispered, "It'll be a wonderful experience to sleep tonight inside this pipe as there's no rain! Star-night or not, we want the coins! And hell with the star-nights, after all, we aren't allowed to go there! We the scum of this country…..!" The old man said bitterly and spat out.

The boy was in an entrancement! He did not hear the words of the old man. He cried joyfully, "Wow! What an illumination! The whole place is decorated with thousands of colorful lights!"

"So what?" the old man said sadly. "It's utter darkness that my fate has given me!" He murmured as if in a soliloquy.

"See, grandpa! What a crowd it is! It's just like a temple festival!" The boy crawled out of the pipe to get a better view of the crowd. Standing on his toes, he stretched his neck as far as possible.

"Ha! Ha! That's only for those who have eyesight, my little boy!" The old man made a meaningless laugh. He did not even know that the boy was not at all listening to him. He coughed aloud and spat out a blob of sputum.

"Grandpa! Standing on this pipe, I can see the whole thing! If only I were allowed to sit in front of the stage and see everything! But entrance to the meeting is given only to those who have taken tickets for the show!" There were tears in his eyes.

"Oh, then, they would have sold tickets at least for a total of one thousand rupees, wouldn't they?" The old man said in a surprised tone.

"One thousand rupees! Oh, this grandpa doesn't know a thing!" The child felt much irritated. He continued with some pride in his voice, "Each ticket costs one thousand rupees, you know, grandpa! And for many of them who took the ticket, one thousand means just one rupee!"

"Perhaps, it'll be a harvest for Appu, tonight!" The old man said hopefully.

"Oh, no!" The boy shook his head in sadness. He continued, "Brother Appu isn't going today for selling peanuts. His child's suffering from high fever!"

"Poor boy!" The old man heaved a sigh and said, "When the date-fruits ripe, there's ulcer in the crow's mouth!" He continued in a dejected tone, "If only he came I would get at least a beedi to smoke!"

"It's all started, grandpa! The meeting! The star-night! There are a lot of people from the cinema world! They all wear full-suits! They look as if they all came out of the cinema screen itself!" The boy could not control his excitement.

The old man felt quite bored. He called out in an angry voice, "Stop your prattling and chirping, you monkey-kid! Come inside the pipe and spread this sack here! I feel too sleepy....!"

The boy ignored the words of the old man. His face was beaming in the light that came from the stadium. He said loudly, "Here comes Brother Appu! Hullo....! Where's your four-wheeled barrow on which you used to sell peanuts, Elder brother?" The child enquired anxiously.

"That's all sold, my little boy!" Appu said indifferently. "Didn't I take the ticket for the star-night with that money?" Appu's eyes seemed looking for someone else...!

"Appu! Why did you buy the ticket for the star-night?" The old man shouted sitting inside the pipe. Then he said, half to himself: "Don't wish for those things which fate has denied to the poor....!"

"I didn't buy it willingly, old man!" Appu seemed to be quite irritated by the moralization of the old man. He snorted, "When those policemen and the tax collectors of the municipality ask you to buy a ticket, you can't escape simply like that. If you don't buy tickets, not only you lose your peanut-barrow for keeping it in an unauthorized place but also you'll be in the jail on false allegations by the next morning, don't you know that....?"

"Whatsoever you got the ticket, didn't you? Now see, the meeting has started. Hurry up and enter the stadium." The boy was very happy in getting a chance, at least, for one among them to see the great event!

"Hell with the ticket! I'm ready to sell the ticket for half its value! But nobody is there to buy even at a lesser amount! They all queue up to buy tickets at full value. But when we are ready to give it at a lesser amount, they become suspicious! If I get at least ten percent of its value, I'm ready to sell it. That will help me to buy medicine for my child! Let me go! I've to sell it before the meeting begins....!" He walked away hurriedly and disappeared into the crowd as if maddened by utter helplessness!

"Grandpa, the orchestra has started! Can't you hear their song?" The child began to hum together with the song that came through the loud speakers:

> Fill our glasses to the brim,
> Serve the fish and chicken fry,
> Let us eat and let us drink
> And let us sing and enjoy....!

"Why didn't you drink the rice-gruel, Sunny? Put some salt and drink it with a bite of green chilly, it'll be delicious!" The voice of the old man came out from the pipe.

The boy didn't listen to what the old man said. He talked as if somebody was listening to him, "Can this town afford this number of cars? How palatial their cars are!"

"Boy! Don't forget to tell Appu to fix this pipe tomorrow.

See, it moves this way and that way!" The old man coughed and spat out. He murmured, "That scoundrel Appu didn't give even a beedi to smoke!" With much irritation, he continued, "Sirrah! Come here and lie down on this sack. Tomorrow we have to suffer all the heat of the day at the bus-stop near the Big Church. You'll be tired if you don't get a good sleep!"

"Please, grandpa! I won't come tomorrow!" The boy talked in a self-assertive tone. "Yesterday, the policeman said that if we begged in front of the Big Church, he would put us in jail!"

"Where else do we go, my child?" The old man sighed in utter disappointment.

The boy, looking towards the stadium, cried out: "Look! Grandpa! The police are chasing away all those who don't have money to buy tickets for the star-night! Alas! They may be chasing even poor Brother Appu!"

"Didn't I tell you to come inside the pipe, you dirty boy! If not they'll chase us too!" The old man said fearfully.

The boy was also frightened. He crept into the pipe, spread the sack-sheet and lied down hearing some playback singer who opened his mouth as wide as possible to present a revolutionary song:

> My dear folks, my dear brothers,
> Who can't afford even one time food
> Or a piece of cloth to cover your loins,
> Let's unite and fight, here we come for you...!

"Oh, grandpa! Did you hear that? They're coming here to chase us away, as you said...! How sad! How sad it is!" The child sobbed...!

The old man's snoring was reverberating inside the pipe....!

16

FACE TO FACE WITH A NOVELIST

I resigned my job as the editor of a weekly when the press baron, under whom I was working, asked me to serialize a novel written by a best selling novelist. He told me that the said novelist was quite popular among the people as his novels belonged to the so-called people's literature! Moreover, our adversary in the publishing field had doubled the circulation of their weekly just by serializing one of the novels of this pop-novelist!

I would starve to death rather than publish the low-brow literature of this so-called novelist, I decided. Of course, the brutish majority of our citizens who elect our rulers every five years read the novels of this writer of sentiments! There onwards, I began to hate even our democratic government, as it was elected by the same brutish majority. Though I was proud of a government of the people, by the people and for the people, I knew that under such a political system, the intelligentsia was always marginalized and, thereby, it became a government of the below average people, by the average people and for the above average people!

I knew that it was foolishness on my part to resign from that well-established publishing company, but sometimes conscience makes us cowards! Well, I suffered much for that! Though I became a freelancer, I struggled a lot to make both ends meet. I roamed here and there and burnt the midnight oil to get some rare scoops. Many of my friends helped me by supplying a few 'threads', though not out of their sympathy towards me, but because professional reasons did not allow them to work on such risky 'stories'!

On one of those days of my groping in darkness, a famous lady-doctor of my town rang me and told that she had a scoop particularly for me. She said that it had some specific relationship with my resignation! She also said that she had great appreciation for my 'write-ups' and read almost every one of them! Well, sheer curiosity tempted me to meet this 'secret fan' of mine and I fixed an appointment with her.

I took my shorthand notebook and pencil, and went to her house, expecting an interview with her. By the way, I should confess that I did not know formal shorthand writing but I had successfully developed a unique method of 'fast writing'! And instead of an interview with her, she told me about an interview she had with the so-called 'people's novelist'!

As she was a doctor, she talked to me without any typical Indian inhibition, taboo, delicacy or hypocrisy. She told me that her interest was in Arts but she had no choice and took a science subject to satisfy the ego of her parents. It was news to me when she said that love belonged to Arts while sex belonged to Sciences! She pointed out that, as a lover of arts, she had to engage in a few love affairs and that was quite natural among art lovers! Once settled in life, she wished to write a novel based on her experience in love. Moreover, she had read in one of my articles that people write literature in order to relieve themselves of some thorn in their heart! As a busy doctor, she had no time to write it and, moreover, her handwriting was quite illegible just like that of all other doctors!

"At last I have decided to seek the help of that pop-novelist so that he could write a novel based on my pretty long life of love and romance, and fixed an appointment at his house." She said to me and heaved a long sigh.

When she said that her encounter with that best selling author was 'awful', I felt interest in it. She also told me that it was an unforgettable, bitter experience for her and, so, if I could write something about it, it would be an asset to the history of modern literature!

Well, I knew this writer as a manufacturer of an incredible number of novels! He was in the news on the publication of his thousandth novel! He might have run out of ideas by that time and expected to enrich his idea-bank by interviewing the lady-doctor! I asked her to tell the details of the interview so that I could scribble them down to make a sensational story. The lady-doctor began her narration and I my scribbling:

"I entered his room which was much disordered, quite disorganized and awfully untidy, like that of any other modern writer. He was giving a last minute touch to his latest novel which happened to be the first after the success of his earlier thousand novels! Yet he was willing to keep apart a few minutes of his valuable time, as his wife cum secretary informed me while greeting me to the drawing room with an indecent expression of disgust and suspicion on her face! Well, in this part of the country, wives used to serve as secretaries, or did not allow their husbands to keep secretaries from the color-sex, except in the case of our ultra-modern writers!"

The novelist welcomed me to his library and greeted me using all pompous words: "Oh, dear gem of a young lady! These moments which I am spending with you in this workshop will be unforgettable and I am fortunate, for this will be a turning point in my career! Ha! Ha! Ha!"

I noticed that his wife cum secretary was eavesdropping and was watching us through the keyhole! I ignored his rotten

language and lustful laugh and told him once again, apart from
what I had told him over the phone, the reason for my meeting
with him. He was very happy to hear that I was there to enrich
his store of ideas! With a pretended sorrow on his face, he said:
"Ah, my dear beauty! If only you had the ability to write
literature! Alas! Alas! I feel deep regrets at the naughtiness of
Nature that doesn't give eyes to the millipede and horns to the
horse! Ah, woe betide!"

He exhibited too much despair on his face, and it's natural
with such a writer of sentiments! I was afraid that he would
burst out into tears at the very next moment! At first, I thought
of using some abusive words at him! But suddenly, he changed
the subject, thank God, at least I was relieved, as he took a
notebook and a pencil, and said: "Well! My dear young friend!
Please be at leisure to tell me what you have to say! Hi! Hi!
Hi....!"

His idiotic smile entertained me for a while! Stretching his
neck as close to me as possible, he sat there like a fake doctor,
staring at those visible private parts of my body seen just above
the table, heaving deep sighs intermittently....!

I began my story briefly. I said that Jose and I were
neighbors and we went to school together and returned home
together. We used to go to church 'under a single umbrella'
during the rainy season, as some film-song writer said once!
While studying in the high school, we were more attracted to
each other by some unknown and unexplainable emotion! It
might be something like falling in love! A kind of mutual
development of attraction between two persons of the opposite
sex, as the psychiatrists say....! But our love came to an end
when I got distinction marks and he failed in the secondary
school certificate examination....!

Striking on the table with his fist, the novelist cried: "Ah!
What a wonderful plot! I will write a four-hundred-page novel

with this plot! Well! I think it's better to give it a title like 'The Graveyard of Dreams'!"

"Stop it! My story is not yet finished!" I interrupted him and continued: "I studied in the college with science subjects as optional. In my class, there was a very intelligent, but not so smart, boy named Ravi. He was ashamed of his distorted face and was an introvert. I tried to encourage him and I used to borrow his notebooks for my studies. During the lonely hours of nights, his innocent face disturbed my sleep. He belonged to the lower strata in our social hierarchy. Yet he did not leave my heart and I began to love him. We were brave enough to take the decision to break the fences of religions and to shatter the impediments raised by the society. But after the Pre-degree examination, I got admission in the medical college, and he didn't, that our love came to an abrupt end...!"

"Wow! Really amazing! A magnificent plot for my next novel....!" The novelist jumped up and down in excitement. He continued: "It's an age of revolutions! With this thread, I'll make a revolutionary novel of about three hundred pages. With its title, 'Break Laws for Love's Sake', the novel will create a stir and sensation in the book market!"

My face reddened with anger. Please hear the rest of my story, I said impatiently. He once again sat on his chair with a sort of utter restlessness on his face! I slowly revealed the next part of my story: While studying in the medical college, I met Jimmy who was the sports star, students' leader, ragging-gangster and the cream of the college. There was not a single girl who was not afraid of this senior student. But he behaved to me in a friendly and polished manner and, not much to say, the seed of love began to sprout in our hearts. However, after attempting many an examination, he left his hope of becoming a doctor and became a medical representative. Of course, we separated with tears in our eyes, standing under that most infamous mango tree at Despair Nook near the Medical College....!

"Oh, my God!" The novelist exclaimed and said: "What a fantastic plot! This novel will be my masterpiece! The magnum-opus! When it comes out with the title, 'Jimmy, my Darling', it'll become a box-office hit! Ha! Ha! Ha...! This novel with more than six hundred pages will be an asset even for the world of literature! Film producers will queue up before me! Hi! Hi! Hi....!"

I was afraid that the novelist would strip off and run around our table crying 'Eureka! Eureka!' I raised my voice and said: Wait for a moment! My story is not yet over! After getting my medical degree, I joined a government hospital as a medical practitioner. Soon, I fell in love with the senior doctor there, Mr. Mohammed. In fact, I didn't know that he was a married man, and though his religion allowed him to marry many women, I was not ready to take the risk. Fortunately, an unexpected transfer for him to another hospital pulled down the curtain for this love too! Later, my parents arranged my marriage with a college lecturer and, now, I lead a happy married life...!

"Stop! Stop!" roared the novelist. He continued: "What you said now is merely a comedy! The aim of writers like me is to give the readers what they want. Alas! I pity your ignorance of our people's love for tragedies! We are just like the Greeks, you know!"

"Excuse me! Let me ask you one thing!" I said with some hesitation. "Can't you write my story as a single novel? If you divide the story into many novels, each with hundreds of pages, I won't get time to read them all, you see!"

"I don't understand what you are up to!" The novelist cried in utter indignation. He continued: "I am a novelist. My aim is not to write 'Thousand and One Nights' or 'The Vikramaditya

Stories'! My slogan is 'one love affair in one novel'! The success of a novel is not in the number of love affairs included in it but in how far a love affair can be made complicated. Can you keep silence for a while? Let me think over your ideas...!"

The novelist sat there looking into the vacuity for a moment. Then, he began to scratch his head, to check the length of his Bulganin beard, to chew the tip of his beard and to pick his teeth with the sharp point of his lead-pencil. I heard a sound behind the door and understood that his wife was observing all our movements! After a few minutes, he began to speak!

"My dear young lady! I have completed my thousandth novel and I am engaged in the writing of the next one. Yes! My second novel after that landmark of a thousand novel publication will be 'The Graveyard of Dreams' and it will end like this! Mr. Jose, the hero, fails a number of times in the school level examinations and winds up his studies to open a private tutorial college. In this business of selling education, like our charitable religious institutions, he amasses much wealth. Then, the heroine comes to that village as a government doctor and faces many troubles from her former lover. He tries to molest her and blackmail her. One day, Jose meets with an accident and his friends bring him to the hospital where she works. Utilizing this opportunity, the heroine injects poison into his veins and kills him....!"

My body began to tremble at such a ghastly thought! I told him in a loud voice: "Oh, no! It's so horrible! I won't even fancy such a thing!"

"It's simply because you aren't a writer! That's all!" He said in a casual manner and continued: "The ending of the novel 'Break Laws for Love's Sake' will be like this. Ravi, the hero of the novel, leads a pathetic life with sad memories of his broken love. He fights bravely against injustice and inequality.

He becomes a social reformer and a politician who wages war against the anti-social laws of religions. He becomes a member of the Legislative Assembly and, then, a Minister and, finally, the Chief Minister, leading a bachelor's life due to his divine love for the heroine.....!"

I stared into his face, for I could imagine how he would wind up his novel, and roared: "Stop your nonsense and give me peace!"

He didn't heed me but continued as if he were in a dream: "The novel 'Jimmy, My Darling', which is to be my magnum opus, will shock the whole world! The hero and the heroine, who bid farewell to each other in tears under the mango-tree at the Despair Nook, meet accidentally in the out-patient consulting room of a government hospital. The hero, who is only a medical representative, after getting formal permission, enters the heroine's room and describes with a golden tongue the quality of a medicine newly produced by the company in which he works. The heroine severely criticizes his company and even abuses and insults him and takes all the free sample packets of medicines offered by the company and puts them in the drawer of her table! The hero stands there like a beggar expecting a last minute change in the heart of the heroine which turns to be futile as she finally roars like a lioness, 'Get out, Mr. Jimmy!' The despair stricken hero returns to his lodge, locks the door, eats all the medicine left in the sample packets of the company and commits suicide.....!"

I covered my face with both palms and began to sob.....and then....to cry! I whispered to the novelist: "I am losing the balance of my mind! It seems you are going to break my heart and my life....!"

He continued his speech like a sadist: "I don't like your last plot which ends as a comedy. I must change every stage of that story. The heroine, who marries the lecturer, loses her mental equilibrium. During the loneliness of nights, she hears the sounds of cries and gnawing of teeth of her former lovers! Their ghosts perform a sort of devilish dance around her. She, realizing that she is at the end of her tether and finding no other way out, touches the feet of her husband, in the traditional fashion, and comes out of the room by midnight....!"

"Stop! Stop!" I cried aloud and stood up.

The novelist ignoring my reaction continued his words in an indifferent tone: "Well! My dearest young lady! You are the person who blessed me with a number of ideas for my future novels! And therefore, I promise you that I shall show maximum justice to my heroines! Ha! Ha! Ha...!"

My first intention was to spit in his face! But his secretary cum wife opened the door for me and, so, I went out immediately saying 'Thanks' and 'Goodbye' to that sadist of a novelist!

The lady doctor wound up her dictation and I made a sigh of relief. She sat there placing the weight of her chin on the fist of her left hand. "What should a woman do on such occasions?" She said as if to herself, heaving a long sigh!

"In situations like these," I said imitating the voice of the girl in the advertisement for cosmetics, "you can publish this in a Women's Mag! They're ready to publish any rubbish and trash if it's written by a female."

I handed over her the notebook on which my interview with her was scribbled and said: "Best Wishes! Adieu!"

17

THE VENDOR OF TOOTH POWDER

From the extreme end of the lane, the voice of the vendor of tooth powder strains into the street:

"Leejiye…. khareedheejiye…. Moti dhantha manjan…. Hamesha isthemaal keejiye….!"

Take it….buy it….here's Pearl Tooth Powder….kindly, use it always….!

Within a few moments, his gig would crawl into the heart of the city. And as the rush and crowd increased in the street, his voice would conquer all other noises….!

The very old gig of the vendor of tooth powder crept along the street. In fact, it was not a gig but a wooden horse-cart with a canvas hood on it. The small bells tied around the neck of the old horse quarreled ceaselessly. His harsh voice, coming through his rusted megaphone, echoed everywhere in the street:

"Ghoda dheere dheere chaltha hei….; gaadi jaatha hei…., Phir nahim kahana bhai….dhantha manjan nahim mila….!"

The horse walks on very slowly, And the cart moves on gradually, So, don't say afterwards, brother, That you couldn't buy tooth powder!

He used to reach the centre of the city before the crowd thickened and, by some odd moment of the evening, he used to leave! But nobody knew from where he came in the morning or to which place he went in the evening! However, his old dilapidated horse-cart and the old skeleton-like black horse that pulled it were the indivisible part of the city, for many years.

Under the worn-out canvas-hood of the cart, like a breathing skeleton, he sat curling himself into many folds. An old rusted megaphone was stuck to his left hand. His voice that came through it reverberated in the street, breaking the ear-drums of the pedestrians:

"Apani dhanthom ki suraksha keliye, Moti dhantha manjan isthemaal keejiye…!"

For the protection of your teeth, kindly buy Pearl Tooth Powder…!

Torn-out and re-stitched shirt…..khaki pants thick with tea-stains and mud….completely worn out leather slippers…..a tattered brown shawl around the neck….and covering all these, a stinking black blanket over the shoulders….! And that lean but tall man of more than six and a half feet in height, sat in that small gig, bending himself into three or four folds!

His sunken eyes were carelessly watching those pedestrians who passed by his cart. His cheeks were hollowed and stuck to his long oval face. Grey tresses of hair were covering more than half part of his wide forehead. His white teeth, like the teeth of a fresh skeleton, as if an advertisement for his tooth powder, gleamed in the darkness of the interior part of the cart where he kept some utensils for preparing or keeping food. And his megaphone never knew rest and it always roared:

"Leejiye… khareedheejiye…. Moti dhantha manjan… hamesha isthemaal keejiye…!"

His ear-piercing voice never created any response among the pedestrians who passed his horse-cart. For them, that tattered horse-cart and the voice of the vendor that came from it as well as the dust and the stench of the city were all equally unimportant! Nobody had seen someone buying tooth powder from him. Even then, he continued his work as if it were the mission of his life. How it would have been if each one of those who passed his cart had bought a packet of tooth powder from him by spending a paltry amount and had cleaned their dirty teeth! Never did they do so! Instead, they bought, with that amount, betel leaves, areca nut and tobacco, chewed them and made their teeth uglier! What a contradiction!

His ill-fed, black horse waddled along the worn path. Its legs moved forward automatically as if they themselves were familiar with the route! The horse was so lean and frail that one could count the number of its rib bones! From its mouth foam and water dripped onto the road. But the small-bells tied to its neck always made some unnecessary noise!

The vendor and the hood of the cart jerked and swung this way and that way in accordance with the swaying of the eroded and loosened cart-wheels. It seemed that his voice entered the megaphone directly from his throat! That voice of the vendor of tooth powder, like the sound of a coconut shell rubbing against the rock, came out incessantly:

"Ghoda dheere dheere chaltha hei….gaadi jaatha hei… leejiye…khareedheejiye….!"

As the cart moved through the crowded street, almost brushing the teeming millions who never cared to clean their teeth, his voice often turned to a mere cry in the wilderness! Poor vendor of tooth powder! It seemed that he was a man who had devoted his whole life to teach the people the primary lessons of hygiene! His gospel of cleanliness echoed in the street. Though none of the members of the public heeded for his voice, the city neither slept nor woke up without hearing his ear-breaking voice!

A city that changed to the tune of time! Day after day, the rush of the people and of the vehicles increased. Newly constructed buildings altered even the entire profile of the city.

Even then, that harsh voice of the vendor came through his rusted megaphone and broke the eardrums of the people!

But....! Where was that jingling of the tiny bells...? They might have fallen down, one by one, on the road and disappeared! Where was the sound of those horse-hooves...? That poor horse that walked to and fro along the street, irrespective of the scorching summer, the rains of monsoon and the freezing cold of winter, on some day, fell down paralyzed on the road...! Perhaps, its life, leaving its tattered cart and its shattered owner and its own worn out body had gone to some permanent resting place!

At one corner of the street, that old wooden horse-cart waited motionless! Its wheels remained dug into the earth! Its curved wooden nose was stuck to the ground as a support to its body! Termites were busy in making their home over the wheels and nose. But the vendor sat patiently in it, bending himself into many folds and watching the passers-by. His voice came through the rusted megaphone:

"Ghoda margaya hei....gaadi gir padenge...., Phir nahim kahana bhai.....dhantha manjan nahim milaa....!"

The horse is dead; the cart may fall; Don't say later, dear brother, That you didn't get tooth powder!

More than his announcement, it was his incessant cough that came through the megaphone! He coughed, cracked his throat and spat out blobs of yellowish sputum onto the road. His eyesight became very dim and a black color had spread over his white pearl-teeth. But his throat still worked with full power! That voice....which was always ignored by the passers-by.....that harsh sound like the rubbing of a coconut shell against the rock....that noise which became an indivisible part of the city....still echoed:

"Leejiye...khareedheejiye...Moti dhantha manjan hamesha isthemaal keejiye...!"

The wheel of time rolled forward without a halt! The rush and crowd of the city became uncontrollable! The number of motor vehicles out-numbered that of human beings! Those old gigs and wooden horse-carts that plied length and breadth of the street, and the old men who sat inside them bending themselves into many folds, and the ill-fed, skeleton-horses that pulled them jingling their small-bells hung on their necks – all had disappeared somewhere forever!

Where was that voice of the vendor of tooth powder, the voice that echoed and re-echoed from every nook and corner of the city? How could the city sleep without hearing that voice? How could it wake up without hearing that voice? Whose ears could not desire for that harsh sound coming out of the rusted megaphone?

The place where his cart used to rest was vacant. A silence of the cemetery prevailed over there. Where was that voice? Did it mean that the gospel of cleanliness had come to an end forever?

Yes! That was what happened! One fine morning, as no voice came out of the cart, the pedestrians became unusually curious. They crowded around the cart, with coins in their hands, to buy tooth powder. His cold and ghastly body, bending into many folds, was lying inside the cart! The empty sachets of tooth powder were lay scattered around him. Not even a spec of tooth powder was seen anywhere in the cart. As he could not bear his hunger, he had eaten all the tooth powder left unsold with him!

The municipal laborers took his body, together with his cart, towards the public crematory, outside the city. His cart served as his bier! Still that rusted megaphone remained tangled among his numbed fingers! They broke the useless cart into pieces and made a pyre with it. The cart and the megaphone, together with their owner, became food to the fire.

From somewhere, the painful neighing of a horse strained towards that burial place and reverberated for a moment in the atmosphere!

Wouldn't that harsh voice still rise in the street of that city? For some, it would be a mere illusion! Some others ignored it! But in the ears of most of the pedestrians, that voice continued to echo:

"Ghoda dheere dheere chaltha hei, gaadi jatha hei....Phir nahim kahana bhai....!"

The horse walks on very slowly, And the cart moves on gradually, So, don't complain later, dear brothers.....!

Author's note: The vendor's words are in Hindi. Non-native English readers may change them into their own mother tongue and feel homely.

18

THE DOWRY-TRAGEDY
AND A FEW OLD SAYINGS

I laughed at my friend when he said, like an old saying, that higher education was an impediment to marriage. But by the time I learned the old saying that experience makes man a teacher, I was too late!

As an educated man, my too long journey in search of my dream-beauty was quite boring. On the first occasion of 'seeing the girl', I liked her but she did not like me. On the second occasion, she liked me but I did not like her. And the old saying was that if you missed two, the third one is definite! The third occasion of 'seeing the girl' also failed as both of us did not like each other.

At last, on the fourth occasion, I discovered my dream-beauty, a sort of love at first sight as the old saying claimed. Soon we fixed our marriage, of course, by simply exchanging the message with our eyes!

Well! An old saying in our place was that both giving dowry and accepting dowry were crimes! But when a bull was brought to draw the heavy cart, was it not reasonable to pay something to the former owner who bred and nurtured the animal? Moreover, I was an educated man, and not mere Adam of the Eden Garden foolish enough to extend instantly both of my hands and accept the forbidden fruits!

When matters reached to such a stage, her father recited the old saying: "Let her continue her studies!" Her father was so adamant on his old saying that my father affectionately permitted me to keep her as wife in my dreams, until she completed her studies!

And, unlike the ordinary young men of our place, it was not difficult for me, as an educated man, to build for us a pretty huge castle in the air!

Of course, another old saying was that an educated man should not be too innocent and straight forward! What exactly happened was that an illiterate young man, introducing himself as a high-salaried employee in the Gulf country, promised her father to marry her without any dowry!

Well! 'Educate a girl until a suitable proposal comes' was an old saying, and her father was adamant to it. Could the crow snatch away the black berries kept all these days as mine alone?

Alas! Alas! What should I say about the culmination of the story! No doubt, there was wisdom in all old sayings! I could hear only an old saying echoing in my ears: He, who stood leaning against the mud-wall, took away the girl!

Author's Notes: For engaged marriages, 'Seeing the girl' is a custom in which the boy and the girl see each other for the first time, usually at her house. Once parents of daughters in Kerala preferred boys even with a menial job in the Gulf countries to locally employed educated boys due to the vast difference in their salaries.

19

A SIMPLE CURE FOR PIMPLES

As a patriot, I had to ponder over a myriad of problems faced by my country and, of course, one could not ignore the fact that our politicians who had no sense of planning created more and more problems every day. Though they were incapable of solving such problems, a few among them, pretending loyalty to the people, sought easy and quick methods to solve them and spontaneously filled the hole with darkness. In their hurriedness to establish the Ramarajya or the ideal kingdom, they used to forget the fact that they would be striking the axe at the very root of eternal values. My experience from Mr. Sriram, undoubtedly, would teach a lesson to such upstarts who were foolish enough to set fire to the ancestral house for fear of rats.

One day, after shaving my face, I was using a foreign lotion gifted by my brother and, suddenly, I noticed a pimple on my face. It was bigger than those pimples that usually appeared on the faces of young men and women who were about to leave their adolescence. This one had become larger, or more swollen, day after day, as my razor ran over it every morning. Whatsoever the reason, I did not care much about it at that time.

After a few days, while shaving my face, I remembered about that pimple and ran the razor very carefully over it so that the blade should not peel it. However, I noticed that it had swollen a bit more and acquired the size and color of a cherry fruit.

As days passed, it not only became larger but also began to irritate me so that I had to scratch that part of my face with a sort of sadistic pleasure. Though I knew that even the caressing or pressing of pimples with your fingers would make them bigger, the pleasure I got while doing so had been tempting my fingers and they moved over the pimple on my face instinctively.

Of course, while shaving my face, thereafter, I was very careful with the razor that it never touched the pimple. Nevertheless, within a month that pimple on my face had grown quite larger and turned red in color, and stuck to my face like an untimely ripened plum fruit.

I should admit that pimples were not such a serious illness or disease like smallpox or malaria, and that one or two at the right place might have the impact of natural beauty spots. But the trouble was that the irritation and pain caused by it spoiled our enthusiasm for working and, at times, even the interest for living peacefully in this world.

And I was not surprised when my wife brought to my notice a write-up on cancer published on that day's newspaper. The appearance of such write-ups was quite natural in a country like India where doctors, both physicians and surgeons, serving especially in the government hospitals, who, instead of conducting proper medical check-up of patients to diagnose their diseases, wasted their time by arranging useless seminars, conferences and symposia on illnesses varying from common cold to AIDS, and like petty politicians, acquired satisfaction by reading the news items on them with photographs which they could bring to the limelight by offering non-vegetarian feast and alcoholic drinks to the local journalists.

Well! I read or rather learned, more or less by-hearted, the whole article on cancer, as I realized that the pimple on my face was disturbing my wife more than me. In that write-up, a doctor with the superscription of his name and address had pointed out that chances were there for pimples, warts, scars, abscesses and swellings to be transformed into cancer, if not examined and treated properly by a doctor. As I was not ready to take risk, and as my wife's compulsion was beyond the limits of nagging, almost a sort of nuisance, I went to a government hospital and showed my pimple to a good doctor.

The doctor made a detailed check-up of my pimple and said with a smile, "There's nothing to be worried; you need just a simple operation. Once you are neatly shaved by Sriram, the barber of this hospital, please come to the operation theater."

He took a piece of paper and scribbled a formal note in his most typical handwriting and handed it over to me. I took that paper immediately to Mr. Sriram. He stared at me in a frightening manner and, pointing towards an ugly chair, cried in his hoarse voice, "Sit there!"

After a long search, he managed to find half-piece of a blade which he put inside the razor-handle, and began to shave my face with an expression of 'how simple all these' on his face! Though I was a person who never gave my face to anyone else to shave, for I did it myself, I sat on the chair grinding my teeth with pain and irritation.

I might have writhed or moved a bit with pain, I didn't know what exactly happened, with a jerk his blade cut the pimple on my face, bringing out blood and puss. He placed a wisp of cotton over the wound and asked me to rush to the operation theater.

As soon as I reached the operation theater, the doctor examined my face and, to my surprise, burst into a vicious laughter. Then with a nod of understanding, he said, "Sriram is capable of doing miracles! He is so talented that every time he reduces my workload. Look, he has completely removed your pimple; what you need now is just an antibacterial ointment and few days to cure it!"

I returned home happily, thinking about Mr. Sriram who had saved me from the horrors of the operation theater and from the pimple which was irritating me and my wife for about a month.

After that incident, much water had flown through the holy river Pamba. One day, my wife who had been born and brought up on the banks of the Pamba, came towards me with a new tiding. That time, the topic for the doctors' seminar was family planning!

My wife, as usual, began to nag me to go to the government hospital and meet the concerning doctor. In fact, she believed the slogan that 'we are two and we have two', as if it were taken from the Bible! She reminded me every now and then how much we would suffer if the number of our children increased above two. In short, I decided to meet the doctor and conduct the vasectomy operation. Of course, it was the most infamous Emergency Period in India, and everybody took immediate decisions quite recklessly.

After examining me, the doctor said with a smile, "There's nothing to be worried; you need just a simple operation. Once you are neatly shaved by Sriram, the barber of this hospital, please come to the operation theater."

The word 'Sriram' suddenly struck my head like thunder out of the clear blue. I felt as if an atomic bomb exploded just below my belt. Somehow, I managed to run out of the hospital and reach my home.

Reaching home, I collapsed on my bed with exhaustion and dizziness, and spent a whole week in fever and high temperature. Later, I came to know from my wife that while I had been in the stage of delirium, I talked even strange things in my sound sleep so that my neighbor, a Pastor, declared that I was blessed by the gift of glossolalia! Moreover, many times I called aloud the name 'Sriram, Sriram' that the Vicar of our church came to me and, placing the cross over my head, said that the ghost of some Hindu had entered into me.

Whatsoever it might be, even these days, whenever I heard the word 'vasectomy', I saw the face of Mr. Sriram, as if he were staring at me through a broken mirror, and felt the laughs of the doctor reverberating in my ears, and with a sudden dizziness, I used to fall unconscious.

Though I knew that my fainting was merely psychological, wouldn't I become a laughing stock to those who heard about it? And if somebody, realizing the reason behind my peculiar illness, denied himself the vasectomy operation, wouldn't his action make the population problem a bit graver?

Therefore, I wouldn't say anything about this psychiatric problem even to my wife. Of course, my wife used to compel me to go and meet a doctor specialized in diseases related to human head! But I could not go to him for fear that he would say I needed a simple operation on my head, and that there was nothing to be worried about it, and that I should come to the operation theater once Mr. Sriram, the official barber of the hospital, did the shaving!

Of course, it was the Emergency Period in India when people took reckless decisions quickly to prove to the authorities that their 'loyalty' was more than the 'king'!

Author's notes: I wrote this in 1976, as part of my novel The Haunted Man, but kept it aside feeling that its humor would mar the general tone of the novel. 'To show loyalty more than the king' is a saying in Malayalam meaning 'to stoop more than what is necessary to please the authority'.

20

WHERE IGNORANCE IS BLISS

"**Woman** is born free but everywhere she is in chains," he said, fixing his eyes somewhere at a remote corner of the ceiling. His tone was serious, and I wondered what was going on in his mind. Well, he used to spoil our pleasant evenings with such unnecessary philosophical comments!

"What's the matter with you, Mr. Modern Machiavelli?" I asked him in a humorous way, to change his depressed mood.

"You don't understand such things, you Mr. Chronicle Bachelor!" He barked at me, with an air of anger and despair. "I'm a father, the proud father of a girl-child, and you can't imagine what my nightmares are!" He continued.

"Well, my dear friend, you think too much! And your thinking won't make any difference to the course of life," I said with clear indignation at his insinuating comment on my personality.

"I'm sorry, my friend!" He said in a pleading manner, and continued in a melancholic tone. "What I mean is a woman's life is insecure even in this modern world! Despite all these boastings on their freedom and empowerment, the truth is that her life, in total, is an utter tragedy."

"Of course! Life is a tragedy for those who feel and it is a comedy for those who think!" I quoted in a sarcastic manner.

"What I say is just plain truth! I don't care what an outsider feels or thinks!" he said in an irritating tone. He stopped for a minute and continued, "I am a father of a girl-child, and a husk-fire is burning inside me, and nothing on earth can put out its red-hot embers!"

"Well! I understand the sentiments of an Indian father!" I said in an amicable tone. "But don't forget that the civilized society all over the world gives equality for men and women. And parents can't keep a girl or a boy for a long time under their custody!" I said.

"Of course! I admit my drawbacks as an Indian father!" he said, catching up with my silly comment on Indian sentiments. He continued, "An African father or a European father may not care much if his daughter goes wayward in accordance with her whims and fancies. He thinks of her promiscuous friendship and lustful behaviors as mere biological needs! Many of them even consider the premarital pregnancy of their daughters as a part of experience in life. Most of them are not morally hurt even if their daughters degrade themselves into public latrines, by having intercourse with several men! They don't care whether their daughters marry or not, or if they're married, whether they stick to their husbands or divorce and remarry! But in India, as you know, sex is not merely a biological need! It is because, unlike animals, human beings can control themselves and lead an ascetic life if they wish so. And sex is a life force, something divine, something that binds the whole society!"

"Of course, one can do anything in this world provided that one must be ready to face the consequences," I pointed out. "Perhaps we give undue importance for character! Where character is only a matter of circumstances, nobody bothers over the consequences of their indiscriminate actions!" I said in a philosophical tone.

He seemed a bit relieved of his stress. He said in a low

voice, "You see, my friend! Before the marriage of my daughter, I was worried whether she would fall in the trap of some lecherous flirts or skunks who take advantage of her innocence. After her marriage, I am still worried whether her husband is capable of giving her perfect family life, with a sweet home where they could give, take and share happiness."

I interrupted him and said, "Of course! If they love each other, everything turns good."

"Nonsense!" my friend retorted. He continued, "Love is merely an abstract term; one day you feel love to one person, another day another person! Love is merely an obsession, a sort of infatuation of the crazy minds! But happiness is something different. Any fool can gibber of his or her love, until one of them finds a better suitor! But true happiness is something unique; it's the outcome of responsibility and obligation, rights and duties, allowances and sacrifice! What you call love only exists between two persons but happiness sprouts from a family atmosphere where individual life is an indivisible part of the society."

"Of course! Man is a gregarious animal," I said with a smile. "But that doesn't mean that individual freedom is thwarted at the cost of social freedom," I continued.

"Well! I agree to a certain extent!" he said with a sinister smile. After a while, he continued, "Perhaps in communist countries, an individual may be a peg in the machine. And in countries under religious fundamentalism, individual freedom means unconditional surrender to natural laws, whether political, religious or biological!"

I said, "Of course, man is a social animal, but at the same time, he is also a rational animal who controls himself from the pulls and pushes of natural instincts. In politics, religion and sex, you see the exercise of physical power rather than mental power. You may oppose this fact, because politics, religion and sex have spiritual connotations from time immemorial."

"Well! Spirituality is the best way to impose power without much opposition from the subjects," he said. "Politics, religion and sex are social institutions in which too much freedom of the individual will lead to anarchy, chaos and confusion. Therefore, whoever breaks the law must be punished."

"I understand what you say," I said. "An individual can become a traitor but within himself. He should not say it to another person that he's against the ruler. In religion, he can become an atheist but don't disclose the fact to anyone else! But how does sex come under this category?" I asked.

He said with a smile, "It's quite simple. Man and woman are part of a social system, and if two persons join, there forms a miniature society. When there's sex between them, the society is automatically involved. Of course, one has the freedom to masturbate or engage in similar sort of personal enjoyments, and it is just like becoming a rebel or an atheist."

"Thus, a person who marries a girl, without following the conventions of the society, is liable to be punished with capital punishment. Same is the case with a rebel or an atheist, isn't it?" I asked.

"Yes!" he said emphatically. "But there are some differences. If a rebel is punished, he may become a martyr for the next dynasty of rulers, or for the next political party that comes to power. But when an atheist is punished, nobody will remember him, as the brute majority of the people are shamelessly blind theists. And the person who marries without following the social norms will suffer from the spouse's community, then, from his own community and finally from his or her own spouse."

"Well! Like birth and life, death also is a grace! If human life in itself is worthy, why should one bother about others?" I asked. "Let the person live or die, starve or martyred, in all cases his life is worthy of living. Follow the law of nature and live an ordinary life is quite easy for an animal; but man is an adventurous animal!"

"You talk like a believer! Of course, one risks his life to save it! It simply means that the person who tries to save her or his life ruins it, as Jesus said." He made a hollow laugh.

"That's why I took the decision to become a fool! Where ignorance is bliss, it's wise to be foolish because it's foolish to be wise where people believe in the dictatorship of the ignorant majority who always rationalize superstitions and false beliefs in the name of culture and tradition," I said with an air of indignation.

"Well!" He said after a pause, "Once you realize that the past has given us a lot of irrational notions, you'll be on the horns of a dilemma! But don't forget that your rationality is tentative, because what one calls rational may be irrational for the other! And as a rational animal, every individual tries to rationalize even the most irrational belief, especially if it is part of some pseudo-legacy! And we forget conveniently to pray for a heaven, 'where the clear stream of reason has not lost its way into the dreary desert sands of dead habit'. He quoted the lines from Tagore.

"No more am I in confusion!" I shouted with joy. "Once you surmount the spur of your soul and gain the courage to become a fool, and to ignore the indomitable urge to say the truth according to your rationality, you are saved! You'll be as cool as cucumber; a sort of a sneering smile will always be hung on your lips; life will be felt as light as a feather; no more heaviness for the mind, no more headache of thinking! You come to the basic philosophy, 'eat, drink and be merry, tomorrow you may die', together with your routine prayers and greetings, 'if God willing.....!' And without any prick of conscience, you can join the song of the witches, 'Fair is foul and foul is fair.......!'"

I bade farewell to him and walked away humming a folk lullaby.

Author's notes: Once you decide to become an advocate, you have to compromise with fancy, but in a world where fact is stranger than fiction, it is better not to make such a compromise.

21

WHO SHOULD CAST THE FIRST STONE?

The premises of the court were fully crowded. A pin-drop silence, in the literal sense of the phrase, prevailed everywhere. All the doors and windows of the courtroom were jammed with curious faces. The members of the public extended their necks as much as possible into the room and strained their ears for the words of the judge. They stared at the judge, at the defendant's advocate and at the policewoman who stood like a statue by the side of the defendant's box, one after the other.

It was the day of the judge. The statement-taking of the witnesses as well as the arguments of the public prosecutor and the defendant's advocate were completed on the previous day itself. And it was the day posted for the final judgment!

The judge was carefully turning the pages and meticulously correcting the errors in the typed verdict to be announced soon. At times, he dipped his steel-pen in the inkpot placed before him on the table and marked something on the margin of each page. And he did not pay any attention to the indifference of the defendant or to the anxiousness of the advocates or to the emotional state of the members of the public who waited impatiently outside the courtroom.

In fact, I had no courage to look at the face of my client. And I sat there, carelessly turning the pages of my useless case-file. Other advocates, who restlessly waited to hear the verdict on an exclusive case in which murder and prostitution combined, passed their time relaxing on their chairs, caressing or scratching their heads or faces and talking in a hushed voice to those who sat on either side.

And my client, the defendant, completely tired of the too long court proceedings, appeared like a patient after a heavy stroke of epilepsy. She stood in the defendant's box like a statue, fixing her eyes on my face. The seams of her carelessly worn white sari moved lightly at the force of the ceiling-fan that slowly turned above the head of the judge. The disheveled curls of her uncombed hair lay scattered around her wheat-complexioned neck. The long, lean fingers of her hands remained tightly clutching over the dirty, black bars of the defendant's box.

Silence was thickening in the court premises. Suddenly, the judge withdrew his eyes from the pages of his verdict and looked around the courtroom in a self-satisfied manner. Then he turned his face towards me and asked: "Is there anything more for the defendant's advocate to inform the court?"

I stood up, made a nod of respect at the judge and said: "Let the sinless person amongst us cast the first stone at her!"

"No need to remind you that this is a court of law," the judge said, staring at me with a cunning smile.

When I sat down on my chair, he turned towards the defendant and asked her in a heavy voice: "Is there anything more for the defendant to inform the court regarding the crimes of which she is accused?"

Resting her chin on her chest, with drooping eyes, the defendant said in a low voice: "I don't deny any of the crimes accused against me. I am a harlot and I am a murderess. I engaged in adultery both for money and for pleasure. I murdered my sick husband by stamping on his chest. Therefore, the honorable court may be kind enough to grant me the capital punishment. Hang me until I die!"

It did not take much time for the court premises to turn into a noisy dais of hushed voices and exchange of hot words and arguments. The judge took the gavel, struck three times on the table and cried: "Order! Order!"

Again a sort of pin-drop silence spread everywhere in the court premises. The judge, ignoring the defendant's words, took the papers in his hand and read aloud the relevant parts from the verdict, including the accusations of the prosecution and the law-points related to the crimes.

He raised his head from the papers and looked around for a while. Then he continued with a smile: "In this case, the defendant has voluntarily admitted all the crimes accused against her. However, the post mortem report points out that the death of the defendant's husband was caused by stamping on his chest by someone wearing a shoe commonly used by a male. And the forensic expert asserts that the said shoe was the product of a very famous shoe-company of our country. But, until now, the police could not produce this valuable evidence before the court. Therefore, the prosecution failed to prove beyond doubt that the defendant had committed the accused crimes."

Most of the people in the court then cast a secret glance at their own shoes! But the policewoman alone, without any expressions on her face, stood dutifully by the side of the defendant's box!

The judge continued his reading: "Yet, as the defendant admitted herself that she had committed the accused crimes, the court strongly suspects that the defendant is suffering from some mental disorder. It seems to the court that the defendant has lost the ability to identify the seriousness of the situation and, even, individuals and facts. Therefore, the court's decision is to send her to some reputed mental hospital for special treatment."

With a triumphant expression on his face, the judge looked around. Suddenly, the defendant who was standing all the time with a bowed head, raised her face, stared into the eyes of the judge and shouted aloud: "Does the court say that I cannot identify individuals because I am a mental patient? If so, how could I identify that Mohammed is the name of the police officer who arrested me, Joseph is the name of the public prosecutor who accused crimes against me and Raman is the name of the judge who made a verdict on me?"

Complete silence prevailed everywhere and the members of the public sharpened their ears to hear the words of the defendant. After taking a long breath, she continued: "Does the court say that I cannot identify facts because I am a mental patient? If so, how could I identify that there are black moles on the thighs of the police inspector who arrested me, of the public prosecutor who accused crimes on me and of the judge who made the verdict on me?"

The voice of the defendant echoed in the court room. All the people in the court premises stood for a moment in utter shock. The faces of the advocates, of the police officers and of the members of the public turned pale and ghastly. But the policewoman alone stood indifferently by the side of the defendant's box!

After a few moments of silence and shock, the court premises once again became lively. As the noise of the members of the public turned too loud, the judge banging the gavel three times, cried: "Order! Order!"

Again silence spread everywhere in the court. Staring into the eyes of the defendant, the judge said: "The court gives one more opportunity for the defendant to prove that she is not a mental patient and she can identify individuals and facts. Can the defendant identify the policewoman who is standing all the time by the side of the defendant's box? Have you identified that her name is Kapalika? Have you ever identified the fact that there is a black mole on her right breast and a red one on her left thigh?"

The policewoman's face turned pale like a white sheet of shroud. The defendant stood for a moment in utter confusion. Then, she bowed down her head and said in a voice of total helplessness: "No!"

The judge laughed aloud and said: "As the defendant is proved to be a mental patient who cannot identify individuals and facts, the court acquits her of the charges against her. The court adjourns for lunch."

The judge stood up and walked towards his chamber. All advocates, police officers and the members of the public turned into statues! A sort of silence of the cemeteries hovered over the court premises!

Author's notes: My profession as an advocate helped me to write a number of stories in which I could blend facts with certain gothic elements.

PART THREE

Selected from Stories Written

After the Dawn of the Third Millennium

22

POLES APART ON THE SAME BED

Unlike me, my friend was a pragmatist and he always tried to solve every problem, domestic or otherwise, in a realistic manner. Unfortunately, I was an optimist, a blind believer in the motto, 'all's well with this world' or a dreamer who always expected only good from fellow human beings.

Gradually, I realized that I was gliding towards a sort of real indifference not only in professional life but also in personal affairs or, to be explicit, towards a sort of placidity or numbness even in my conjugal life! Perhaps, this was common among all optimists but many of them survived due to their strong faith in certain pseudo-sciences!

In fact, I was in between the devil and the deep sea, between optimism and reality, and I really needed the help of a pragmatist. And one day, he was there in my house, as if you were looking for a rare herbal medicine and, all on a sudden, you found the same creeper-plant twined on your leg!

As usual, he broke the ice cursing the ways of modern age and complaining about the lack of fidelity among present-day couples. Whenever we get free time, we used to talk on different subjects, and this time it was 'divorce'.

"Patience, that's the only means to survive!" He declared, and added, "Of course, it must come from both the partners!"

"Marriage takes place in heaven", I said solemnly,

suppressing my real feelings. I knew that my words would easily provoke him.

He laughed aloud and said sarcastically, "Then, we are all angels, perhaps, to ignore our unique problems and always pretend to be happy!"

I ignored his joke and argued in a serious tone, "But, of course, children bind a marriage, don't you accept it?"

My comment was the last straw that broke the camel's back. He stared at me and cried, "No! Not at all!" he continued in a harsh voice, "Children can be born even without a real conjugal life; it's only a natural process!"

His face turned reddish and he asked me, distorting his mouth in an ugly way, "Aren't we persons of individualities, with separate entities of our own?"

I felt his temper; of course, he belonged to that group of people who were annoyed easily. I winked at him and said with a cunning smile, "Well! It is said, perfect sex solves all domestic problems".

"Who said that?" He cried, "Freud? Nonsense! Sex is only a biological need and it happens quite automatically. Of course, sex can enhance the intimacy in conjugal life but it is not inevitable! Even in physical union, don't we feel, at times, poles apart, like creatures from two planets? If there's no understanding, the net outcome of a sexual act is merely a sense of loss!"

I knew that he was cleverly avoiding the word 'love'; a safe word for an ideal optimist. I laughed aloud and said, "Sense of loss and sense of gain! Do you think that the husband and the wife are mere business partners who calculate the profit and loss after every amorous act?"

My friend kept quiet and I thought that he was wordless at my eloquence. I resumed with an air of victory, "See! There's an island in the east where there is no divorce among the married people. The Elder will order his soldiers to take the quarreling couples in a boat to a lonely rock in the mid-sea. The soldiers will return to the island, leaving the stripped-off couples on the barren rock until they mend themselves their relationship".

I continued, "Every morning, the soldiers go to the rock and call aloud, "Did you forgive each other and forget your arguments? Have you settled your dispute and agreed to live together?" If the answer is 'no', the soldiers return leaving the couples on the cold rock for another chilly night. It is said that the couples will be ready to return by the third day, for how could they suffer the chilly wind on the rock for more than two nights?"

My friend burst into laughter and said, "That's quite practical! What the couples need today is a common enemy! Of course, you can forgive but you can't forget! It's funny how you try to mix water and oil!" He left my house with a smile lingering on his lips.

I sat quite silently for a while. As far as I knew, my friend was leading an ideal life. He and his beautiful wife were working in a government office, drawing a pretty good salary on the first of every month. Good food, good clothes, good house, good jobs and good friends! What else was needed for a happy married life!

Only God alone knew how much I struggled to make both ends meet! My poor wife was always engaged in domestic duties like cooking food, washing clothes, looking after the children and a lot of endless, non-remunerative works! However, within a few years, with my limited salary, I could buy cooking gas-cylinder, washing machine, refrigerator, television and other equipments to make her life comfortable. As far as I was concerned, I did the same exhausting, monotonous work with the same salary! Of course, I felt a sort of jealousy towards her, although she always made the usual complaint, 'I've only a pair of hands!'

It was a shock for me when she told me one day, "How lucky you are! Every day you go out and meet different people in different situations, while I sit idly at home. How boring is my monotonous routine of work in the house! I am jealous about you!"

How could my friend understand the seriousness of the estrangement we felt in our hearts! Of course, we knew that it was all silly. It's only a misunderstanding, just a simple matter that would be solved within no time! Yet, somewhere in the depth of our reason, we were hearing the ringing of a death knell!

We were living under the same roof, in the same room! We were sleeping on the same bed, on the same soft mattress! We were lying under the same blanket, inhaling one another's warm breaths, hearing the lullaby of each other's breathing! We were in each other's embrace, feeling the warmth of our bodies! But didn't we feel, at times, worlds apart, just like strangers hailing from two different galaxies?

Until one day, early morning, my friend came to my house and said, "At last, it happened! We got divorced!"

Author's notes: One of my poems published in *Blossoms, An Anthology of Poems* - p.133 (Writers' Forum, Ranchi, 2001) has the same title and the poem is also included in my collection of domestic poems, *Magic Chasm (2007)*. I made an experiment with that poem and converted it into the above short story with a different ending; and it appeared in www.chowk.com on 10th February, 2011

23

THE JUNCTION

I was returning from abroad after successfully completing my work contract for two years with a foreign ministry. At the airport, I expected my wife to receive me and take us home in a car brought from my home place which was a usual practice among us. Instead, to my surprise, I was received only by my sister and her husband!

Perhaps my wife was still angry with me, I thought.

In fact we had a petty quarrel, something like a mere misunderstanding, that was quite common among married people, and such quarrels usually ended up in a better harmony. She felt that as a husband, I had not 'cared' for her! The word 'care' might not be appropriate. It meant that I had not loved her sufficiently or protected and looked after her properly or, even, sat near her day in and day out lightly caressing and rubbing her body or talking or listening to those silly issues concerning our relatives and neighbors! Such simple quarrels, as you know, were regular among husbands and wives who loved each other sincerely and, as a writer, I did not give much importance to such complaints raised by my wife, especially, as we had been leading a marital life for a quarter of a century. And, moreover, she presented this issue before me, rather in a serious tone, through a letter, only after my leaving for abroad so that I did not get an appropriate chance to patch up the matter face to face. But this was not, of course, a genuine excuse to abstain from coming to the airport to receive me!

My sister told me, instead of going straight home, we should first go to a nearby hill resort where they had rented two rooms, one for them and the other for me and my wife, and that my wife was already waiting in that room. My brother-in-law pointed out that it would always be better to go home after patching up the difference between my wife and myself. My sister added that there was a very famous church on that hill and her favorite saint there would be a better mediator for us. My brother-in-law supported her and said that there was also a beautiful lake at the foot of the hill where we could sit and talk and solve all our family problems since I had returned for good.

We reached the hill resort after a ride of about two hours, and my sister and her husband went to their room leaving me at the front of the room where my wife was waiting for me. Perhaps, they did not like to encroach into those private moments of our meeting! After a gap of two years we were meeting and I expected a dramatic scene with much excitement, embracing, smiling, sobbing and what not. But to my surprise, she was still in an angry mood, rather indifferent, and did not care even to talk to me. Frailty, thy name is woman, I mused.

Soon my sister and her husband knocked at our door and said that they were going to the church and asked us to follow them along the road on the right, for the other road on the left was going down the hill towards the lake. Let the couples go ahead first, and then we follow them keeping a safe distance for our private talks, I thought.

A few moments later, I saw my wife hurriedly going out of the room, without uttering a single word to me. I had to wash my face and change my dress, after that long car journey! I was ready within two or three minutes, and locking the door, rushed out to catch up with my wife. I could not find her anywhere and I thought that she might have run towards the church road to join the company of my sister.

The church was at the top of the hill, and I felt some difficulty in climbing up the road as fast as others, or as in my past days. When I reached the church, my sister and her husband were waiting impatiently for us. I looked around to see my wife but she had not reached there! My sister suggested that my wife might have, by mistake, taken the left road that led to the lake. My sister insisted that the church was the right place for our compromise. I asked them to wait there so that I could go down the lake road and bring her with me.

I hurried down the hill and reached the junction where one road went to our hotel and the other further down the hill towards the lake. Walking down the hill was quite easy for me, and I reached the lake in doubled up pace.

Fortunately I saw my wife sitting by the side of the lake, and heaved a sigh of relief. I did not ask her why she had taken the wrong path, for it would intensify our quarrel, I thought. I told her that others were waiting at the church that we also should go there. She was still angry and was reluctant to come with me. She told assertively that I could go and bring them to the lake. If I tarried on there, those at the church would become too anxious and scared about our whereabouts. Moreover, the words of my sister had created a mysterious sort of optimism in me that I too believed that the church would be the right place for our conjugal consensus. But finally, due to her adamant nature, I decided to go to the church and avoid further confrontation with her before a prospective happy reunion!

I started again to climb up the road to the church. Walking up and down the hill had already exhausted my energy that I could walk only very slowly up the hill road. One side of the road was a deep valley or, rather a steep gorge-like cutting. A few meters before the junction, I noticed a white shawl lying by the side of the road. As it was not there when I walked down to the lake, or I might not have noticed it in my hurriedness, I looked at it with curiosity. Beside the shawl, I saw a piece of ornament, which looked like a brooch or a locket, not of course, of gold for gold ornaments would not have that sort of dull, corrosive appearance. I took it in my hands and observed it wondering how they would appear there. Owing to my climbing up the hill, I was panting heavily and I could very well feel even the palpitations of my heart!

Suddenly I saw three persons running towards me from the junction. They stood around me and looked at me suspiciously. One of them snatched away the ornament or the curio from my hand and asked: "Where did she go?" He, like a wrestler, quickly turned my hand to the back and twirled it as if to pluck it out of my shoulder socket! Before I could reply him, the other man asked: "Where did you hide her?" As I stammered to answer him, he gave on my face a hard knock with his powerful boxing fist, quite unexpectedly, and I felt blindness creeping into me! The third man, like a judo master, kicked at my groin, with a shriek usually made by people who practice martial arts. I fell down unconscious!

When I opened my eyes, I found that I was lying in a hospital. The smell of chloroform and other medicines nauseated me. I saw my wife anxiously watching me and she smiled through her tears, heaving sighs of relief and joy. I gawked at her with the defeatist state of mind. I could not find my sister and her husband anywhere, and my wife told me to relax and sleep again.

Gradually, I came to know many more things! First, that I had lost the sight of my right eye beyond recovery; second, that my right hand was amputated as puss had entered into the bone; and third, that I became totally impotent due to the scrotum kick of that judo master. Moreover, I was lying unconscious for a week and, as my sister said, just before going back to her place of work, that it was a miracle through the mediation of the saint at the hilltop church, with whom she had regular contact in prayers, that I could get back my life. Also I came to know that all these days and nights in the hospital, it was my wife who looked after me.

I looked at her face helplessly, knowing that the doctor had revealed to her everything related to my present condition. She smiled convincingly and said: "At least now you'll be with me all the time!" Of course, I wished in such a situation, she would leave me and, then, elope with some other man to some other place. I could only smile in a cynical manner. How could a disabled person like me, give proper 'care' to her, when I even miserably failed to give it to her throughout the past twenty-five years?

If I stop my story here, my readers who have blind belief in morality will be provoked in their genuine indignation to throw stones at me, and so let me continue with it, for my left hand is sufficient enough to type the letters on the computer, or even to do better things!

After three months of hospitalization, I took my discharge from there. I told my wife that I would like to take rest alone for a month at the hill resort and she agreed to it, as she believed, that it would give me opportunity to adjust myself with my disabled condition. Looking at the mirror, even I myself could not recognize me, as many changes had occurred to me during those three months. I became very lean, my face was all grown with thick beard, and with one eye and a hand lost, I looked quite a stranger even to my dear relatives!

I went to the hill resort and took a room there for a month. Within a week, I made friendship with the waiter, the cook and the gardener there and cleverly enquired about those three men - the boxer, the wrestler and the judo master. They told me that those three men used to come and stay in the hotel every alternate month, and during such periods a pimp brought them new, young girls to share their beds, for such adjustments were quite common in tourist hotels.

"It's in business, you know!" They said, expressing their helplessness. "Three months ago a girl escaped from their custody, 'and no one knows what happened to her', and those three became so angry that they left the hotel immediately," one of the cooks said. "And on their way, they even turned an innocent man into pulp," the gardener added.

A few days later, a car stopped in front of the hotel and out came the three – the boxer, the wrestler and the judo master. They entered their specially-reserved room after giving order to the waiter to bring three glasses with two pugs of whisky and soda water and a plate of mutton fry.

I went into my room, took a stripe of sleeping tablets given by my doctor to use on sleepless nights if necessary, and powdered them fast. Keeping it in my pocket, I entered the kitchen where the waiter was preparing the dishes as per order. As he was frying the mutton pieces, I offered my help to arrange the drinks, and he was very happy about it. While pouring the liquor into the glasses, I managed to put the sleeping powder in it without being noticed by the waiter.

After a few minutes, the waiter took everything to their rooms and served. By that time, I took a hatchet used for chopping mutton in the kitchen, and hid it under my shirt, safely screwing it under the belt. Then the waiter returned and said with a smile that they would not drink much then as they had business to do in the evening. I heard them laughing and merrily drinking and talking loudly about their previous experience with girls and about the girls whom the agent promised to bring for that night. After a few minutes, all of them became silent!

Pretending that I was going back to my room, I formally thanked the waiter and managed secretly to enter their room. All the three were lying either on the sofa or on the bed, snoring under the effect of the sleeping pills. I took out the hatchet and neatly cut off the boxer's right hand, then both the hands of the wrestler and then the judo master's right leg. Of course, two of them made groaning sounds, as everyone does in sound sleep.

Taking all the four pieces on my shoulder, I rushed out of the room and went straight to the place where I had seen the white shawl and the ornament. One by one, I threw the limbs into the gorge, like holy offerings to the owner of the shawl. Then I came back to the junction and waited there in a sort of dilemma till I saw the gardener of the hotel coming that way. I told him to go to the hotel urgently and make arrangements to take the three inmates to hospital so that they should not die.

I looked at the two roads, one leading up to the church where I would be once again saved by my sister's saint, or up and up and up to the top of the hill and to the skies; and the other leading down to the lake, and then, down and down and down to the depth of the lake. I preferred the latter.

24

THE HEAD-LOADER

He was walking fast, carrying the heavy box of highly explosive gun-powder on his head. His only aim was to save his wife and children from the imminent probable catastrophe. But in his hurriedness, he did not notice the gun-powder that was leaking out from a hole in the box, making a line of it on the road behind him!

Hurry up! Hurry up! They encouraged him, cheering up at his speed. He also heard them laughing aloud!

He looked back for a moment. In order to speed up his efforts, they had already set fire at the other end of the gun-powder line!

For a moment he thought of returning to them with the box so that everything would end up altogether. Soon, he cursed himself for thinking in such cruel terms. He desperately tried to throw the box away and save himself but it was glued to his head. The more he struggled to pluck it away, the more it stuck to his head.

He felt completely exhausted and he heard the whole world laughing at him. He ran forward, ran and ran, realizing the stream of fire fast approaching from behind....

25

THE BIER BEARER

As you were walking towards the only shop near your house, for a 'smoke' to kindle the flames of your imagination, on that Second Saturday afternoon, you came to know that a young girl's dead body was found in the unused quarry-pond, just a few meters ahead of the cart-road where the goat-path from your house joined it.

Out of sheer curiosity, you went to the quarry-pond where a few of your friends and neighbors were standing anxiously by the edge of the pond, talking in a hushed voice. You had a casual look at the body which was floating face downward, as if it were looking down into the depth of the pond. You asked them who the girl was but they could not give you a clear answer as none of them could recognize the identity of the body without seeing its face.

You felt a sort of guilty conscience that turned into real indignation. For you were also one among those members of the local Citizens' Forum who signed below a long complaint and submitted it to the 'authorities concerned', pointing out the possible dangers of such an unused quarry-pond, and the necessity of filling it up with soil. Of course, the contractor who took cart-loads of granite slabs from the quarry had agreed to fill it with soil, once the work in the quarry had been completed.

Your house was just about a hundred and fifty meters away from the quarry-site that you happened to be one among those who had brought an abrupt end to the breaking of stones at the quarry where they used highly dangerous explosives. Though the contractor could mint money by selling the granite, he left the quarry without filling it with soil, following the stay order from the court against using explosives there which would be damaging to the strength of your house.

During the rainy season, the quarry was filled up with water, and you thought that the pond would be of some use to someone or, at least, to some domestic animals. But as months passed, it became the breeding ground for frogs, snakes and mosquitoes. Moreover, the naughty children of your neighbor-hood had put some fast-growing African water-weeds that covered the surface of the water within no time! And the condition of the quarry-pond worsened when many of the fast-growing African cat-fish, kept for fun in the garden-pond of your neighbor, jumped out of it and slipped with the rain-water into the quarry!

Of course, on every Second Saturday, you used to sleep like a wooden log, even up to ten or eleven in the morning, and your only daughter used to go to her office early in the morning without disturbing you. It was your habit to enjoy 'full freedom' on such days in a completely relaxed mood, by waking up an hour before noon, by brushing your teeth for a long time as if nothing else to do, by taking the cold breakfast prepared by your daughter and kept covered on the dining table and, then, by scribbling down those foolish reveries, dreams and nightmares that had been haunting your mind for a week, slowly sipping your favorite Planter's Punch or Bloody Mary, until your daughter returned from her office by five thirty or six in the evening.

On that Second Saturday, after taking a few sips of the

cocktail and writing about two paragraphs of a new short story, you wished to smoke a cigarette and, as you could not find one in the packet, you decided to come to the small bunk of a shop from where you used to buy your favorite brand of cigarette.

As you were standing by the side of the quarry-pond, without knowing what to do, you heard one of your friends commenting: "It's impossible to identify the body! The cat-fish might have finished the face and fingers!"

"Well! Our Kerala State stands top in the world in the rate of suicides but that doesn't mean that every person should come to our quarry-pond to commit suicide!" Another friend expressed his disgust and indignation.

"Did anyone inform the police?" You asked with the seriousness of a responsible citizen.

"Yes! Early in the morning, we sent our retired policeman to the town! Who else is daring enough to go to the police station?" One of your neighbors said and laughed aloud to reduce the tension prevailing among the by-standers.

"It's almost time for the police to come! We must clear-off the place lest we should be spoiling our life answering all the queries of that khaki-uniformed sons-of-a-hung-man!" Another neighbor said with genuine fear.

"You're right!" A third one supported him and said: "Every working day, we'll be asked to go to the police station where we have to wait on the verandah like criminals until the Inspector finds time to call us into his room! He'll ask all sorts of foolish questions in his police-language, as if we have raped, murdered and thrown the body into the quarry-pond! Why should we hold the tail of a tiger?"

While most of the spectators gradually moved away from the quarry-pond, you and your friends moved towards the shop, down the cart-road, and stood in front of it, smoking cigarettes one after another, and waiting for the arrival of the police.

After a few minutes, you saw the Head Constable coming along the cart-road on his bicycle. By seeing the khaki-uniform of the policeman, almost all your neighbors and other spectators withdrew themselves into their hideouts!

You and your friends greeted the Head Constable in the most polite manner. He enquired about the case, twirling his thick moustache casually, and asked a few questions, even to the old shopkeeper who was unnecessarily trembling head to foot at the sight of a policeman! The Head Constable took a notebook and pencil from his pocket and jotted down certain points necessary for his First Information Report.

Then, he turned towards you and your friends and said: "What's your idea! Shall I leave the carcass to be decayed for the next two days, spreading stench all over the place? You see, today is Second Saturday and not a single policeman is ready to attend the case! I came here just because of the request made by that retired PC who was my senior in service! And tomorrow is Sunday, as you know, and nobody will be there in the station. If you are ready to cooperate, we can take the body to the main road, from where I shall arrange some vehicle to take it to the hospital for post mortem. What do you say?"

You and your friends discussed the problem and decided to help him on humanitarian ground. Moreover, to keep a dead body stinking in the quarry-pond near your house was unthinkable! You knew that it was wise to kick the ball into the other court!

The Head Constable turned towards the shopkeeper and asked him in a rough voice to give a thick knife. The old man quickly handed over the knife with which he used to cut areca-nuts!

The officer looked around and saw a laborer standing at a far distance. He shouted at him and asked him to come nearer. He gave the knife to the laborer and asked him to make a temporary bier, by cutting down some branches of a tree. The poor laborer seemed to be very proud in helping a police officer!

After a few minutes, he gathered two long poles of equal length and a few sticks. He placed the poles on the ground side by side and the sticks as cross-bars over them. He tied them properly with pieces of coir taken from the shop. A long jute-sack was spread on the temporary bier and another plastic-sack was folded and kept on it to cover the dead body. When the bier was ready, the constable asked him to take it to the side of the pond.

You and your friends also followed them to the pond. But when the Constable asked the laborer to take the body from the pond, he hesitated for a moment. Then, you and your friends offered to pay him some money and he agreed to do the task.

With the help of a wooden pole, he drew the body to the bank and all of you helped him to place it on the bier, covering it with the plastic-sack. The face of the body was so damaged that you could have only a quick glance of it before it was covered. You turned your face away, took some money from your pocket and gave it to the laborer so that he could buy some local drinks to forget the mess!

Soon, you and your friends took the bier on your shoulders and walked down the cart-road about a kilometer away from the quarry-pond towards the main road, from where the body could be carried in a motor vehicle to the government hospital for post mortem. And the Head Constable walked ahead of you, pushing his bicycle!

As you were all moving along the cart-road, carrying the bier on your shoulders, you were singing the familiar song in a very low voice: "In the Chariot of Time.......!" And you walked briskly as if you were participating in a very solemn ceremony!

You were walking in the front row where the head of the

body was placed, keeping one end of the pole on your left shoulder. By the time you walked half of the distance towards the main road, you began to feel a strange attachment towards the person whom you were carrying. You felt as if you were bearing the bier of a dear relative of your own blood and marrow! In order to keep away your strange thoughts, you began to sing rather a bit loudly: "In order to see my native land, all alone I am going......!"

One of your cousins walking with you was keeping one end of the other pole on his right shoulder, and he said in a complaining tone: "Ouch! Once you die, your body doubles its weight! It seems my backbone will break soon!"

You ignored his comment. In fact, you felt only as if you were carrying a feather on your shoulder! You were walking with firm steps and felt a sort of rhythm in your onward movement. You feared that your quick walking might disturb the dead body of the girl as her head was swinging sideways in accordance with your movement. With your right hand, you took the handkerchief from your pocket and, even, placed it as a support for her head!

A long tress of her curly hair was dangling down from the bier and water dripped from it. As you were walking, it was swinging and, at times, water drops from it fell on your face. Those water drops flowed down your cheeks mixing with your own sweat. You felt even the light fragrance of her hair and wondered how that girl's hair acquired a smell quite familiar to you!

Some kind of an unknown fear was passing through your mind. You continued to walk as if you were in somnambulism! As you reached the main road, the Head Constable asked you all to place the bier by the side of the road. You delicately placed the bier on the ground, as if placing a flower on the altar of a deity. You wished to have a closer look at the body but you were afraid to do so.

You quickly turned back towards the cart-road that led to your house. You did not even say a word of 'goodbye' to your friends. A lightning passed through your heart! A heavy thunder was rumbling in your brain! A tremor passed through your spinal cord! You walked hurriedly towards your house, striding, hopping and running; quick-breathing, panting and coughing; tired, exhausted and thirsty; wondering in stark anxiety whether your only daughter had returned home or not....!

Author's notes: I loved to write my stories in First Person Narration but made this experiment in Second Person Narration to please my literature students.

26

THE ICY DECISION

Once he took the firm decision, he felt a sort of perfect peace of mind. No more was he on the horns of a dilemma; no more was he in confusion! No tension at all! A completely relaxed mood! Somewhat like the equanimity gained through deep meditation of a long period!

Such a mental condition might be very rare. It was a kind of indifference or a feeling of vacuity. He was no more a human being with sentiments, sensitiveness and sensuousness. He was like a robot controlled by some built-in chip! Every action was automatic, pre-planned and fixed. Nothing could change his decisive movements!

It happened all of a sudden! He was not like that on the previous night. Then the night was thick dark, and not a single star appeared in the sky. Black clouds marched along the sky threatening every object on earth. Rumblings of distant thunders and flashes of many a lightning filled the air! A heavy storm was blowing, rattling the window panes. And it was a blind-man's night!

He heard a glass window beating against the wall. His daughter was so careless to close the window, he thought. The heavy wind that came through the window forced even a door to creak in a terrifying manner! Even doors were not closed!

What happened to her? Silly girl! He thought.

Of course, early in the evening, he had a quarrel with his daughter. She was so self-assertive and adamant in her decision. She wanted to marry a vagabond! Funny! Marry a person below her social status, far below the status of her family! How could she think of such an impossible thing? Marry a person with an entirely different culture! A person who belonged to a totally different background; different in race, in language and in religion! And how could a sensible father allow such an immature decision of his only daughter?

Well! Nobody gave much importance for such things in the modern age! Many people thought of marriage as an affair of two free-thinking individuals and a license for the sexual life of the concerned persons! Did it mean that a marriage had nothing to do with the culture of the society to which they belonged? Did it mean that conjugal life had no special sanctity? Anybody could preach philosophy when the problem was not theirs!

He could not imagine such a marriage for his daughter! He knew that if two culturally different persons married, there might occur certain very particular problems in their private life. At the early stage, the couple might ignore them in the heat of their blood! But such meticulous traits of behavior could not be explained as they happened differently, at different occasions! And he was sure about the existence of such situations in family life. They were inevitable in such cases. And in a male dominating society, only the female would be victimized!

Of course in the modern society, youngsters think that marriage is only an affair between a man and a woman. Men, especially voluptuous men, became experts in trapping women with their flirting. In ancient days, it was not so. Only men were warned against the mouth of strange women. Lest the scripture should have been like this: The mouth of a strange man is a deep pit, she that abhorred of the Lord shall fall therein.

He could not think of such a pathetic stage for his daughter. She was his dream! Her future had been his only concern for quite a long time. He lived all these years for her happiness. He saved every coin he earned and saved it for her happiness. And he could not ignore the honor of his family. But his foolish daughter appeared to be too blunt in her decision. Of course, foolishness is bound in the heart of a child, as the scripture says, but she was too grown up for him to use the rod!

Did it mean that they truly loved each other? If so, nobody could change the sincere intention of young people, especially in these days! Even there were the stories of Romeo and Juliet and of Laila and Majnu who sacrificed their life following their blind belief in sentiments! Moreover, he knew that calf-love was a biological matter among the tribal-people and a psychological issue among the civilized. In his daughter's case, it should be the latter which needed some real counseling and, if necessary, a medical treatment.

A few weeks earlier, she had told him, "Dad! All my hostel-mates are feminists! All are mere psychiatric cases!"

Then he did not understand what she meant by the word 'feminist'! He always thought of it as a great movement among women to raise their status in a male dominating culture. He knew that there were many generations in feminism as it was in the computer revolution! It was said that certain feminists in the western countries did not care for marrying the opposite sex! Perhaps, his daughter was tortured by her hostellers. Or even her roommate might have made some disgusting or irritating advances! In order to escape from that mess, his daughter might have sought the help of a boyfriend or of a person whom she knew! He might have threatened or warned her roommate or hostellers, and thus helped her in some way or the other!

But he knew that no man would help a woman without selfish motives! In order to avoid her roommates, his daughter might have talked and walked together with that boyfriend. And he might have well-utilized the opportunity by introducing her to his friends or relatives, for taking some of her photographs and gradually leading her to a vortex! Of course, a friend in need is a friend indeed! But if that friend is from the opposite sex, definitely, there would be a purpose for his help! Or he might have misunderstood her friendship as love!

That's the problem with the oriental culture, he thought. No girl could keep friendship with a boy! No woman could have friendship with a man of any age! Every male had only one intention, the selfish motive to exploit the situation! And the innocent girl or woman had to face difficulties for her frankness!

One day he asked her, "My dear little child! Tell me openly! Do you love him?"

"I like him," she replied, looking into his eyes.

"But.... What does it mean? What I asked is 'Do you love him?' Cut it straight!" he said, raising his voice.

"I like him!" She replied in an ice-cold voice.

"Do you mean that you like to marry him?" He wished to get a clear answer from her.

"I don't care!" She replied without any change in her voice.

He was further confused at her answer. She might be telling a 'divine lie'! He again asked her, "Does it mean that you don't care whether you marry him or not? In that situation, how did this question of marriage come between you and him?"

"Perhaps he likes to marry me," she said indifferently.

"Do you mean that he is compelling you to marry him? Or do you mean that he is blackmailing you?" He asked her in a peaceful tone.

"No! We're friends!" She replied calmly.

"Do you say that there's nothing more than friendship between you and him?" He asked in a relaxed tone. "But our culture doesn't know about such a relationship. In fact, friendship in between men and women in their marriageable age is a taboo here."

"I don't care!" She said curtly.

He stopped interrogating the girl. How could he explain the situation to her? Poor girl! She didn't know the male point of view on such matters! Perhaps no parent could understand the sanctity of true friendship in between male and female. For a male, at least in our culture, friendship is useless and a waste of time unless it suffices his selfish motives. Of course, philosophically, with a cunning smile we all agree to all such ideals, for we knew such things as simply impracticable!

Perhaps, the guy was blackmailing her! He might be prepared to go to any extent. If a male took a decision to acquire a female, he could easily break all the impediments through fair or foul means! Once acquired, he would feel victorious, as he could throw her away at any moment into the street, something like waste material! Once she was thrown out by him, she could only be accepted in the ghost farm, just like any other used or secondhand things, and that was the so-called great culture of our country! If the male was clever and fluent in flirting, any female could be convinced and trapped, for he could easily apply the usual techniques like pretensions and disguises, dramatic actions, sweet words, promises and handsome offerings, self-torturing, blackmailing and even threatening of the third degree! And the innocent female would be hooked at last!

The next morning he was ready for a journey. He took his air-bag and came downstairs. His daughter looked at him questioningly, as he said 'Goodbye' to her.

"Where are you going?" She stammered.

147

"Just to see him and to ask him what's his idea." He said carelessly.

"Then....?" She looked into his eyes.

He felt a bit irritated. He tried to control his feelings and said in a cool manner, "If he is incorrigible and if there's no way out, I'll kill him!"

"Oh, no!" She shrieked. After a moment's silence, she said in a pleading tone, "Dad! He was my friend. He helped me in my dire need. Otherwise I would've become a mental patient by now! Such was my situation in the hostel! He is an innocent guy. He misunderstood me and imagined like any other young man under similar circumstances. You can't punish him for his good intentions. Instead I would prefer to die myself!"

Her words were so powerful that he returned to his room, without uttering a single word. More words lead to more quarrel! But how long could a father remain silent in the house with his daughter who lived in the adjacent room? Silence too widens the gap in relationships among married couples!

On the previous evening, he talked to his daughter about it and the argument led to a serious quarrel. She was not ready to tell the whole truth. Perhaps, she had no confidence in her father! Or she might be mesmerized by that street-boy's showings off! How could a sensible girl of such a high status fall victim to the tantrums and gimmicks of an ordinary person, about whom she knew nothing at all?

"It's my mistake! It's all... my mistake! I must be punished! I must suffer! I must die! I must die!" She just lamented, instead of answering his questions, resting her face on his chest.

She was like any other woman, he thought. They would prefer death rather than telling the truth about their failure! When they could not find themselves a solution to their problems, instead of admitting their inability, they preferred to commit suicide! But what was that mistake, she talked about? If she committed a mistake, as her father he also would be responsible in a way. But how could he extract the secret of her heart! He decided to talk to her in a more convincing manner. Perhaps, she would open her heart, he thought.

The storm was howling like a frightened wolf. The creaking noise of the door irritated him. He came out of the room to close the windows. He noticed that his daughter had forgotten to close the door. Through the cleft of the door he saw a candle burning on her table. He knocked on her door. There was a quick movement in the room, a rustling noise and the candle suddenly went out. He pushed the door open and entered the room. In the darkness, he saw the frightened figure of his daughter. He took out the lighter from his pocket and lighted the candle.

His daughter was standing by the side of her bedroom like a statue. A plastic rope with a noose at the end was hanging from the dead fan. There was a letter properly folded and kept under a paperweight on the table. He snatched the letter and read it under the candlelight.

The letter said: "Sorry, Dad! Death is the only permanent solution to the problems of a person. You may think that I am a silly girl! I've read many stories about people who died for the sake of love. But here is a death for the sake of friendship. Martyrdom in the name of friendship, for the first time in the history of our culture! No one else shall be blamed for my death. I am fully responsible for it....."

He raised his head from the letter and looked at his daughter. After a moment he said, "Do you think that you alone are responsible for it? If I am responsible for your birth, I must be responsible for your death too. Come here, my dear child!"

He extended his arms towards her. She slowly came towards him. There was no sadness or tears on her face. He wished to embrace her and console her but she stood a few steps away from him and asked, "Can't you live alone?"

"No!" His reply was harsh and adamant. She knew his nature; he never changed his word!

After a moment's silence, he asked her in a low voice, "Can't you live until my death?"

"No! I've decided!" Her words were solid. He knew her nature; she was his daughter!

He stared into her eyes. She avoided his stern look by turning her face away from him. She took an envelope from the table and handed it over to him. It was a letter addressed to her, a registered letter with that day's date-seal on it. From the cover he took out a letter and a photograph. He unfolded the letter and read it. She had underlined a few sentences and his eyes fell on them.

"I give you 24 hours. After that this photograph will appear in all newspapers. As a warning, it is already on the internet. Copies are also sent to all your classmates."

He looked at the photograph; his daughter stands with a man, as if they were married couples! "Nonsense!" he cried. "Anybody can manipulate a photograph! And just for this crime, he should be punished!" He seemed a bit excited at this new turn of events.

"No!" she said. "He may be a criminal but once he saved my life. And now, don't try to change my decision!"

After a few moments, he said in a cool voice, "Do you mean that death is inevitable?"

"Yes!" she replied. "Even Jesus died for the sins of others, didn't he?"

"Well! That means both of us must die, do you agree?" He asked her in a hard tone.

"No. Not necessary. You've years to live!" There was a sort of sadistic pleasure in her voice.

"I'm too old to have another life with a wife, somewhere in the remote countryside and to bring up a daughter." He said as if he had taken some adamant decision.

She shrugged her shoulders and said, "Well! It's all up to you....!"

After a moment's silence, he said, "Yes! I've taken the decision. We'll both die; I'll kill you first and then I'll follow you. But give me 24 hours! Let me think about the mode of our murder and death. Until then, leave everything to me, agreed?"

At first she looked at him suspecting some foul play. Soon she felt the power of determination in his eyes. She came towards him and kissed his cheek. And he moved out of the room and slowly closed the door of her room.

He went into his room and sat on the easy-chair. The whole night he was thinking about different types of murders and deaths. Many scenes of murders, from the primitive murder of Abel by his brother Cain, crushing his head with a big stone, to the modern electrocution of a mafia chief, flashed through his mind. Quick death by arsenic finally entered his mind. It is very difficult to get arsenic but he knew he could manage it from his former classmate in the school who ran a jewelry shop. Goldsmiths used to keep it and paying a good amount he could easily get it.

The problem was how to administer such a poison to his daughter. Mixing it with food and offer it as her last dinner? Or putting it in the coffee or tea and serve her in a casual manner? It must be in an artistic manner! Suddenly the scene of seeing his daughter for the first time came to his mind.

Years ago, he was waiting outside the labor-room of a famous hospital. He walked to and fro like a caged musk-cat! His wife was admitted into the delivery room and was undergoing the travail. At times he heard his wife's suppressed cries straining out of the labor-room. Moments of anxiety and

151

tension passed one by one. Then he heard the cry of a child and his heart began to throb. He restlessly walked from one corner to the other of the waiting room.

Suddenly the door half-opened and the nurse brought out a small bundle of white flannel carefully kept in her left hand. Among the folds of the white flannel he saw the tiny face of an infant.

"You're lucky! She's so lovely!" The nurse said with a smile.

She was declaring indirectly that it was a girl-child. Of course, every father wished to have at least one girl-child to cry and shed tears when he died! And he knew that only soft-hearted virtuous people got girl-children. But for him she was more than that!

If a child is not born within two years of marriage, everybody will start questioning and smiling! The wife's parents will suspect the impotency of the husband and the husband's parents will suspect the barrenness of the wife! Indeed he was lucky! She was born as a result of his four years of continuous prayer! She was born as an evidence for his masculinity, a proof that he was capable of producing a child!

Among the folds of the white flannel, he saw his first-born, his own replica! Her face was so perfect, without any ugly wrinkles of new born babes. She was staring at him with her bright black eyes! It seemed as if she were asking him whether he was really happy at the birth of a girl-child! Of course, in his part of the country, most of the parents wished to first get a boy-child. But he felt proud of her especially because she had his chestnut complexion, not of his wife's wheat complexion, and she had even his dimples on her cheeks!

His mother-in-law poured some honey from a small bottle into a saucer and gave it to him as was the custom there. He took his wedding ring and rubbed it in the honey. It was customary for the father to give this honey mixed with gold as the first food to the infant. Her lips were dark, thin and tight. He took the ring with a drop of honey hanging on it and touched it on her lips. She opened her tiny mouth and sucked the honey, staring at him or looking into his eyes without even a blink! He remembered that she used to look at him in the same way, with those suspicious eyes, throughout her life!

Thunder cracked in the sky, flashing a new idea into his mind. Yes! That's it! Potassium cyanide gives immediate death! No pain; no suffering! The way of operation was fixed! The next day he bought a small bottle of honey. Then he went to his friend's jewelry shop and managed to get the cyanide.

The goldsmith was afraid at first to give him the poisonous chemical. But he assured him, "It's for a unique experiment in the college lab." When a professor demanded and offered a good price, the goldsmith had no other option!

Flashes of lightning and rumblings of thunders began. He heard the heavy showers beating against the window panes. A shattering storm was howling outside incessantly.

He did not care for such protests from nature. He was doing his work perfectly like an experienced scientist. He took a saucer and put the cyanide powder into it. Then he opened the bottle and poured the honey over the powder. He drew out his wedding ring from his ring-finger and with the ring mixed the honey and the powder very carefully. Taking the saucer in one hand and the ring in the other, he entered her bed-room, like a priest with chalice in one hand and the pyx in the other.

She appeared as if she were in a sound sleep. She had covered herself with a white blanket up to her neck. Her face was calm and quiet. He approached her and sat on the cote near to her head. He took the ring and with it dropped the potion on her lips. She opened her lips and sucked it down. Three times he dropped the mixture into her mouth and she drank it deliciously.

For a moment, he was afraid whether she would open her eyes and stare into his. At that thought, his hand trembled a little. Fortunately, she did not open her eyes. She appeared as if she knew what her father was doing. She made a heavy sigh and he noticed a slight movement of her facial muscles. Then she stopped her breathing.

He moved into his room, like a priest returning to the altar too tired of distributing the Eucharist to a large number of believers. He put the wedding ring back on his finger and sat on his bed ready to lie down. He took the saucer to his lips and drank the rest of the potion at a gulp and fell back, resting his head on the soft pillow.

27

BEFORE THE COCK CREW TWICE

He sat near the fire in the courtyard, warming himself. Though he was a tramp and an outsider, the guard of the mortuary enjoyed his company, especially on those nights when a fresh cadaver was brought to the morgue. On cold nights, the guard of the mortuary used to make such bonfires with waste paper, outdated news-dailies and the white papers issued time to time by the government.

The courtyard in front of the mortuary was a deserted place and nobody dared to enjoy the warmth of the fire there, even on very cold nights, except the guard and the attendants who were appointed to prepare the dead bodies for the next day's post mortem. Moreover, the security police of the hospital had kindly allowed the guard, against the rules and regulations of the hospital, to keep a fire at the courtyard in front of the mortuary, as the guard had convinced them that a fire would drive away the ghosts that came during midnights in search of their bodies! The guard had mercifully allowed him to sit near the fire because he knew that it was always better to keep company in such horrible surroundings!

Moreover, the tramp had already become almost a 'hospital creature', as we, the doctors, used to say about such people who spent most of their life in the premises of the government hospitals where free medical treatment was given.

Early morning, before the queue of patients formed, he would be at the door of the doctor so that other patients could only stand behind him. Every day he changed the doctor in accordance with the changes in his ailments; one day it might be fever that he stood before the general physician, another day it might be chest pain that he stood before the cardiologist and the third day it would be pain inside the knee that he stood before the orthopedics surgeon! And the doctors diagnosed him as a hypochondriac or malingerer, and scribbled in their illegible handwriting some ordinary medicines like paracetamol or vitamin B complex tablets just to please the patient.

It was only a few months ago that he came, like a tramp or a destitute, to that hospital premises. He might have come there from a far away place, perhaps, walking miles and miles, because he looked then so 'haggard and woe-begone'! Rarely did he talk to others, but most often to himself, and that too were quotes from great works in English literature!

He was a man of about sixty years, but by the weariness and despair on his face, a score more years could be added! On the first day of his arrival itself, he had taken an out-patient ticket from the hospital and collected some free medicine from its pharmacy. He avoided crowded areas and, by evenings, came to that mortuary area which others deliberately avoided.

On the first evening, the guard of the mortuary had tried to chase him away as strangers were not allowed to roam around there for security reasons, but finally, finding him a harmless psychiatric case, perhaps, with some small nuts loose in his brain, allowed him to spend the nights on the verandah of the morgue. In fact, he was really in need of someone like him to talk to during his night duty, especially just after midnight when the street dogs howled incessantly, creating an eerie atmosphere.

The guard always talked much in order to drive away the

horror of his duty and he found the tramp a patient, silent listener. He told the tramp that he was doing the work of a guard for many terms because other guards were reluctant to take up the work of guarding dead bodies. In fact, they liked to work at other gates of the hospital where they could make some extra money from the patients or from their relatives who tried to enter the wards at odd timings.

The guard brought some more waste paper and the tramp took them one by one, threw it into the fire and kept it going on. It was past midnight and a chill wind was blowing, carrying tresses of mist. A cock crew from a nearby hotel, perhaps, a cock kept for the next day's meals. The guard, as if irritated by the crowing, commented, "Ah, it's time for him to go to the kitchen morgue!"

A dry smile came to the lips of the tramp and he murmured, "Who knows about the play of fate; if it's him today, tomorrow us! Life's a walking shadow…!"

The guard laughed aloud as if he was hearing a joke. Then, he said, as if talking to himself, "Poor man! Nobody for you? No family? No wife?"

"She may be up there!" The tramp looked up into the skies.

"No son?" The guard asked him again, and the tramp kept quite, as if playing on the strings of his weak memory.

"No daughter?" The guard asked persistently. For a second, the tramp's face beamed.

"Yes! One daughter! The credulous girl eloped with a womanizer!" The tramp said sadly. Suddenly he stopped as if words choked his throat. The tramp's lips were trembling and the guard wished to change the subject.

He noticed the vendor-maid who sold black coffee from a carrier-kettle to those whose relatives were admitted in the hospital, and asked her to bring them two glasses of coffee. He used to offer the tramp a glass of coffee in gratitude of keeping company with him during such sleepless nights.

The vendor-maid stared at the face of the tramp and said, "And you also were among the people who brought the girl's body to the mortuary, weren't you?"

But he denied, saying, "I know not, neither understand, what you say!"

As the vendor-maid moved away, the two attendants of the mortuary came there and sat near the fire to warm themselves. Their duty was to prepare the dead bodies for the post mortem. In fact, the duty-doctor never touched such cadaverous things, and used to ask them to break open the skull to take the brain out or to split open the chest and stomach to take out internal organs for the laboratory tests. If dead bodies were admitted in the mortuary, such specimens should be sent for biopsy tests but, usually, in the case of unclaimed bodies, only a report of the duty-doctor would be enough to write the case off.

After a few minutes, the senior attendant asked his friend to warm himself until he checked the body. He said to the guard, "Give me the key to the morgue. I came early because I heard the commodity is young and fresh! And I must prepare the body before the doctor comes!"

The senior attendant snatched the key from the guard, opened the door of the mortuary and entered hurriedly into it. The guard and the junior attendant looked at each other and laughed understandingly.

The tramp took more paper and put it into the fire. He also cracked some dried twigs into pieces and put them one by one into the fire, murmuring, "Life is a tale told by an idiot….full of sound and fury signifying nothing!"

"What? You speak English?" The junior attendant asked in surprise. The tramp kept quiet, looking into the flames that tried to catch the skies in vain!

The junior attendant turned towards the guard and enquired, "No claim yet for the cadaver, is there?"

"No!" The guard said, extending his hands towards the fire. He continued, "Found in the jungle. Might be a case of suicide! Or somebody might have thrown the body in the jungle after murdering her! Poor girl! It seems as if she belongs to a good family!"

"Who bothers?" said the junior attendant. "How could we waste such a commodity? Tomorrow it'll be claimed by the worms!"

Minutes passed, the door of the mortuary opened again and the senior attendant came out, completely exhausted of his work. He took a deep breath and said with a feeling of satisfaction, "Oh, Gosh! She was so tight and full mouth!"

Then he turned towards the junior attendant and said, "Now, it's your turn. Go and check the commodity! And the bottle is kept on the table."

The junior attendant soon entered the morgue. The tramp was trying to recollect where he had read those words for the first time, perhaps uttered by that boorish peasant, after raping Woinitu, the heroine in Daniachew Worku's novel, the Thirteenth Sun!

The senior attendant came towards the fire, rubbing his hands together. Strong smell of spirit came out of his mouth. The guard stared at his face with disgust and snorted, "How could you do it, you bastard?"

The senior attendant laughed aloud and said, "The government supplies enough spirit for that, don't you know old man? Who's going to waste such a good drink on a carcass?"

He crackled his throat and spat a blob of sputum into the fire. Then he turned towards the tramp and stared into his face and said, "How strange! Your face looks exactly similar to that of the stuff inside the morgue! Is she someway related to you?"

The tramp denied it, shaking his head, and said, "Damn it! I don't know the girl!"

He took an old newspaper, crushed it into a ball and put it into the fire. At the heat, the paper spread a bit, revealing the photo of a girl. The guard saw the picture and cried in surprise, "That's the girl!"

Before the tramp could have a glimpse of it, the fire licked it and changed it into a black sheet of carbon. After a few minutes, the door of the morgue opened and the junior attendant came out. He made a crackling noise and said, "Ah, it was nice! Thank you, Senior! You made it easier for me! But, of course, it smelt your shit! Ha! Ha! Ha!"

The guard spat out disgustfully, with a vomiting noise and murmured, "Mother-fuckers! They don't even leave the dead bodies! These nasty carcass-eaters!"

The junior attendant ignored him and turned towards the senior attendant and asked, "What are you going to do with it after the post mortem? The medical students are after me with bundles of currency notes. The Neuro-students want the head; the Cardio-students want the chest; and the Ortho-students demand the hands and legs! What do you say?"

The guard interrupted him and said, "Remember, it's a special case! There's all possibility of a re-post mortem! You'll lose your heads! Don't forget that!"

"Oh, leave it this time, Junior! We'll get some beggars for the students!" The senior attendant said carelessly.

The junior attendant came towards the fire and looked at the tramp as if enquiring whether there would be someone else to share the game! Suddenly, with a surprise, he said, "Surely, you are closely related to that thing, aren't you? The faces are one and the same!"

The tramp angrily retorted, "Damn you! A plague on your tongue! Didn't I tell you, I know not of this girl of whom you speak?"

And then, the second time the cock crew. He felt as if a thunder struck his head; a lightning passed through his heart!

Though I am a doctor who has been accustomed to similar ordeals, I could not write more about that tramp, for tears brought darkness into my eyes. So, I leave his fate for your fancy, but let me wind up my part by quoting what the scripture said, 'He went out and wept bitterly'.

Author's notes: A confession before my readers. After writing half of the story using my favorite 'I' narrator as the protagonist, I felt a sort of ominous emotional stress that I could not go on with it. At first, I did not know what to do. Then, I dared to change the narrator, deliberately blunting the sharpness of the conflict, and completed the story.

28

A CALL FROM THE BLACK CROWS

Power cut, or load shedding as the officials of the Electricity Board call it, that lasted for an hour or a maximum of two hours, was a usual phenomenon in that part of his country. Of course it created inconvenience for the democratic masses as well as for the bureaucrats and the industrialists. Though it was taken for granted that every individual must suffer some kind of inconvenience for holding up the great principle of democracy, situations like unpredicted power failure created many problems for doctors who looked after the people till they died, or for the morgue managers and the crematorium operators!

The Municipal Electric Crematorium was on the outskirts of the city. It was a deserted hillock, full of trees and green vegetation. A muddy side-road reached the crematorium and ended in front of it. Though the municipal authorities inaugurated it claiming it as a landmark in the cultural heritage of the country, the Hindus continued to follow the unhygienic practice of cremating their dead relatives in their own five or ten cents of soil, spreading much stench in the atmosphere and, thereby, making neighbors' lives miserable and unbearable. Christians and Muslims buried the bodies of their dead ones in their respective burial grounds so that for them a crematorium was merely a waste of the public fund. However none of them

162

had any objection in cremating the unclaimed dead bodies or the bodies of those who were murdered or committed suicide, in the municipal crematorium.

In fact, he got the job as the crematorium operator as no one else was ready to take up that job even in that part of his country where unemployment was so severe! The unemployed youth preferred starving to taking up the work of cremating unidentified bodies! Moreover, unlike in other government offices, there was no attraction of bribe or extra income in that particular job.

Of course there was not much work for him. Once or twice in a week a police jeep came with an almost decomposed or mutilated dead body packed in a grass-mat and the policemen or helpers pushed it into the kiln and left the place after getting his signature on certain papers. Or once or twice in a year the body of some rationalists would be brought with much pomp and show and the crowd waited until the kiln started working and then dispersed with satisfied faces as if they had enjoyed a festival till the last part of it.

In all such cases, it was his duty to put on the switch so that the iron door of the kiln would automatically be closed and the cremation process would go on for a few hours until the timer stopped. The next day he entered the room just to collect the ash and deposit it in a nearby pit behind the crematorium.

But if there was no electricity, he had to wait there; sitting patiently on the plastic chair put on the verandah of the crematorium, for neither the policemen nor the enthusiastic crowd could wait for an indefinite time. And that was the most difficult part of his job. On certain days, if the electric supply was not returning on time due to repairing of electric lines or some problems with the transformer, he used to put on the switch of the kiln and walk down the hill for a cup of coffee or tea, so that the cremation process would be started as and when the electricity came. Of course his job was such an exemplary one that no one dared to question his method of working.

However on that day he had no desire to leave the dead body in the kiln and go for tea or coffee, though he had switched on the kiln. It was almost two hours before that police jeep came with the unidentified and unclaimed body of a young woman. As usually happened on similar situations, there was no electric supply on that day too! They placed the body in the kiln and left after getting his signature on some papers.

From their conversation he understood that it would be the body of a girl who had eloped with her lover a few months back. He might have betrayed her and, after taking her valuable things, killed her and thrown the body into the jungle. But there was no evidence for it though there was a possibility that it would be a case of suicide. Who bothered in such cases as there was no complaint on the part of relatives! He did not dare even to look at the face of the body as it would bring bitter memories of his own daughter who had run away with a stranger.

It was the time of afternoon load-shedding and the policemen left hurriedly in their jeep handing over the burden to the crematorium operator. He pressed the switch of the kiln on as usual and sat on the plastic chair and relaxed. Sentiments were not for the crematorium operators but he thought for a while about the condition of her parents. They might be living in the vain hope of their daughter's return as a happy wife and a mother of one or two children!

Of course, elite Europeans or tribal Africans could not understand the real mental agony of Indian parents when a girl child was born to them! Until the child was grown into maturity and was handed over in marriage to a suitable person, their responsibility continued. Till her marriage they felt as if a burning coal had been kept in their breast pocket! Sometimes their anxiety prolonged even after her marriage. Perhaps, such concerns were unnecessary as the modernists think! Girl or boy, as individuals, both should be treated equally, they might say. But whether the leaf fell on the thorn or the thorn fell on the leaf, the harm was always for the leaf, as we Indians used to say.

In his case, it seemed that he had expected such a fate for his daughter someway or the other. It happened years ago when his daughter was only three months old that he had witnessed a sort of epiphany! It was a real revelation to him that he tried not to cry whatever happened in her life due to her own foolishness. He knew that the line drawn on her head by fate could not be rubbed off!

He clearly remembered that horrible incident. On that day, he was returning from his work, quite exhausted by the travel by bus for a score of miles and then a walk for about a kilometer from the bus-stop to his house in the village. As he entered the drawing room of his house, he was shocked to see his little daughter lying on the floor, completely bathed in her excreta! His wife had not returned from the city and his mother to whom they had entrusted the child was busy in the kitchen. In those days diapers were not commonly used for children in the villages, and old people believed that the backbone of the infants would become stronger if they were laid on a mat spread on the floor. And his daughter was playing quite happily, her body completely stained with stinking shit!

He quickly changed his dress and took the child towards the well, calling loudly to his mother to bring water to wash her. She ran towards them and put down the bucket with a rope into the well. She drew three or four bucketfuls of water and poured it over the child. He washed her three or four times with fragrant soap until she was completely cleaned of the mess. Unlike other children who cried when bathed in cold water, his daughter giggled joyfully as each bucket of water was poured over her!

He dried her body with a towel and took her to his bedroom. She was so tiny and weightless that he could easily keep her in his left palm while preparing the bed for her. He laid her comfortably on flannel, sprayed some perfume and sprinkled talcum powder all over her body.

She continued to giggle playfully, staring into his eyes! He became slightly angry or rather irritated while the little one continued to laugh as if she had taught him a lesson!

"You naughty little girl!" he said and gave her a light slap on her thigh. But it made her laugh louder!

"You wicked little brat!" He again said and gave her another slap. She continued to laugh as if she was experiencing some sort of sadistic pleasure!

Then slowly sleep came to her and she became silent. She put her left-hand thumb into her mouth and began to suck it, as she used to do while sleeping. He pulled out the thumb from her mouth but she was so adamant that every time he pulled out the thumb from her mouth, she put it back into her mouth with more force!

Though a little child, how self-assertive she was! He thought about the future of such a girl and cried silently. Then, he took her in his hands and lied down on the bed keeping her on his chest so that she could not suck her thumb. Within seconds, she began to sleep, perhaps, feeling the lullaby of his heartbeats! Tears were still flowing down from the sides of his eyes! It was then that he heard the strange voice, like an oracle: "Be prepared for more tears of sorrow and joy!"

He looked around but he could not find anyone! He could not even understand the meaning of those words. Tears of sorrow or tears of joy? Or tears of sorrow followed by tears of joy as the culmination of the story? Whatever it was, he should be prepared for both! He cried and cried silently until tears stopped flowing from his eyes! He did not say a word about that epiphany to anyone else, even to his wife, but continued to cry and wet his pillows on many other lonely nights! At last he tried to believe that such oracles are made in equivocation, with double meanings and a rational person can easily overcome them. Of course he had an evidence for it; he could trust his heartbeats; they were powerful enough to pacify her disturbed mind and to bring solution to all her problems! He tried to console himself.

Years passed one by one. The more she grew the more she became a stranger to his heartbeats! How long children could be dependent on their parents? She learned her own ways and views about life and found friends of her own choice. His only prayer was that she should not fall into the trap of a flirting womanizer! 'For a womanizer is a deep ditch and a strange man is a narrow pit'. But what he feared happened at last! She eloped with a man about whom she knew almost nothing!

Was it for that, he nurtured and brought up a daughter? Perhaps, she knew everything about him or she believed so! But he was sure that she did not know anything about his family, about his lineage, whether his family had any hereditary diseases or any history of insanity and so on. Of course, these were the main reasons why people preferred arranged marriages to love marriages. Moreover, a wise daughter makes a glad father, but a foolish daughter is the heaviness for her mother, as the Preacher of the Proverbs would have said in this case.

Perhaps she was happy with him, more than with her parents. She was part of his blood and marrow and he had to find out the reality. He should go there and, if possible, make a compromise and invite them to his house. Or he would be keeping her somewhere secretly as a second wife or 'little family' as his people used to call such a practice. If he had betrayed her, it was his duty as a father to punish him. And the only punishment for him was a death sentence which he himself should execute; for it was not a case to be decided by the court of law which delayed action. Justice in personal matters should be immediate; and law delayed meant law denied! Fortunately he had traced the photograph, address and phone numbers of the so-called accused from his daughter's room, after her elopement.

Suddenly the crematorium operator felt as if he had heard a voice, like the cry of a crow, quite nearby from the kiln. He ignored it and looked around. Evening was fast approaching and a cold wind began to blow. He noticed a number of black crows quarrelling with each other on a tree in front of the crematorium, perhaps, to find suitable places for their roosting.

Still there was no sign of electricity! He took a woolen shawl from his bag and covered his head and body. He cursed the irresponsibility of the workers in the Electricity Board. Did it mean that he had to sit there the whole night, guarding an unidentified human carcass? And he had neither appetite for tea or coffee nor for his dinner that was kept parceled in his bag. He felt so exhausted by the day's heat and the mosquitoes were singing a lullaby. Gradually he fell into a deep sleep.

Even in his dream, he was duty-conscious as he had taken the decision to find out the whereabouts of his daughter at any cost. He traveled in a train and reached the town where the so-called accused was working. He knew that he should be very careful in every step. First he went to a readymade shop and bought a Muslim dress, a long kurta, pajama and a white cap. Disguised as a Muslim businessman, he took a room in the lodge, giving a fictitious Muslim name. He contacted the culprit's office and talked to the receptionist in a very friendly manner. He told her that he had come from another part of the country and it was very urgent to have a personal talk with him.

"Then, you may be here to attend his marriage?" she asked.

"Well! Ah, yes! Will you please tell me how to reach the place of his wedding?" He asked without much excitement.

The receptionist told him the details of his house in another town and his phone numbers. Then he asked her in a casual manner, "Perhaps he is marrying the girl with whom he has been living for the last few months!"

"Oh! That girl! She left him a few weeks ago! You know, it's all merely for a fun…just his hobby!" She giggled over the phone.

"Of course, I know his nature! But where is she now?" He asked rather nervously.

"Only God knows! Perhaps, the fate of similar foolish girls! And who bothers about such things?" She laughed aloud as if she had made a joke! A tremor passed through his veins! What did she mean by that? Did she mean the red-light streets in the metropolitan cities?

He checked-out from the lodge with a firm determination. He went to another readymade shop and told them that he was a priest and he bought a cassock usually worn by Christian priests. Changing his dress in the dressing room of the shop, he came to the street. Disguised as a priest, he went to a medical shop and bought a bottle of liquid rat-poison. From another medical shop, he bought a needle and a syringe. He also bought a beautiful garland of fresh flowers from a flower shop. Keeping everything in a plastic shopper, he went to the place of his target.

By evening he reached the place and took a room in a lodge situated in the outskirts of the town. In the name column of the register, he wrote "Rev. Fr.' and completed it with the name of his victim. He placed his shopper in the room and came out. He walked a few meters away from the lodge, took an auto-rickshaw and went to the place of his victim's residence. When he reached the house of the culprit, he asked the driver to go a furlong further. He asked the driver to stop nearby a small shop and went out to talk to the shopkeeper, just to please the driver.

After a while he returned to the rickshaw and asked the driver to take him back to the town. Twice he could see for himself the wedding arrangements, the pandal, the decoration and the illumination. He got down from the rickshaw, a few meters away from the lodge, near a telephone booth. He gave the driver the fare with a handsome tip that he went away without any query. He went to the telephone booth and rang him. Somebody took the phone and he told the name of the person whom he wanted to talk. A minute's waiting and he could hear only the cheerful noise in the house and, then: "Hullo! I'm here!"

Over the phone he said, "Listen carefully! I'm a Christian priest currently staying in room number 301 of the South View Lodge. I have very important news for you from the girl with whom you were staying a few weeks back. It's very urgent and if you don't come, you'll regret tomorrow. Remember room number 301 of South View Lodge and come straight to the room within fifteen minutes. Okay!"

He cut the line quickly and he was sure that the culprit had felt the urgency in his tone. He paid the phone charge and walked hurriedly towards the lodge. He sneaked into his room without making any noise. He took out a pair of gloves and put them on his hands. Then he took the garland from the plastic bag and placed it carefully on the small table at the corner of the room. Then he took the bottle of rat-poison and filled the syringe with the liquid. He placed the syringe on the left side of the garland, hiding it among the flowers, so that he could take it with the garland and use it on the left side of the culprit's neck. He knew that a few drops of the poison, if directly injected into the veins of the neck, would be enough even to kill an animal.

For a moment, he looked around the room. He took the pillow and kept it ready; for if he made much noise, he should smother him to silence. He pushed all other pieces of furniture in the room towards the wall, keeping a big sofa-chair in the middle of the room. Three or four times he did the rehearsals, taking the garland in his hands and coming towards the chair, and perfected himself in the method of his operation. At last a vicious smile of satisfaction came to his lips.

Soon he heard the sound of a motorbike and he looked through the window down at the street. He had seen the photograph of the person and it was he, and he could recognize him very easily. He closed the window and kept the door of his room half opened. He knew that he would come alone, for true criminals would not reveal each and every secret to others. As soon as he reached the door, he welcomed him into the room with a friendly smile, closed the door behind him and requested him to take the chair.

He did not give any opportunity for him to talk and said, "You're on time! First, let me convey greetings from the girl with whom you spent a few weeks. I would like to inform you that she is happily married and lives with her husband in Canada. She came to know about your marriage from a friend and asked me to convey her congrats to you. She also asked me to give you a garland on her behalf."

He went to the corner of the room, took the garland with the syringe hiding in it and walked towards him. Before the culprit could suspect any foul play, he slowly put the garland over his bowed head. As the garland reached his neck, in a split-second of time, he pressed the syringe into the veins of his neck.

As a sudden reaction, the victim tore away the garland, crying, "Hey! What's it?"

"Oh! I'm sorry! There may be a wasp or a honeybee among the flowers!" He said in an innocent tone. He continued, "Please do relax on the chair! I'm really sorry!"

The culprit rubbed his neck vigorously and cried, "Who are you? What do you want from me?"

"Don't shout! Understand!" His voice was harsh and icy. He continued, "I'm the father of that foolish girl whom you sold to the agents of the red-light street! No other girl should suffer from you like this in future!"

It seemed that the culprit wished to call aloud and cry for help but his voice was tangled somewhere in his throat. He felt tired and sat suddenly on the chair. In utter helplessness, he made a cry, "Caw…." And soon, the blood and foam that oozed out of his mouth choked his voice forever.

He took out the cassock he was wearing and dressed the dead body with it. He placed the syringe in the dead man's right hand and placed it near to his neck. It appeared as if the culprit had committed suicide. He placed the empty poison-bottle near the sofa as it had slipped away from the dead man's hand. He took the garland and put it in the shopper. He cleared the room of all evidences of his presence.

He dressed himself as an ordinary person. He placed everything else, including the gloves, back in his plastic shopper. He detached a big rose flower from the garland and pinned it on the cassock near the chest of the dead man as a last homage. He closed the door and came down the stairs. He waited on the steps for a while to see whether the receptionist was at the counter. He could see no one; the counter-man might have gone for his dinner. He sneaked into the darkness of the street and walked hurriedly towards the place where waste materials were burnt. He threw the plastic shopper with all its content into the fire and waited until it burned completely.

He caught the next bus and went to the famous city of Hindu temples. Early morning, he tonsured his head, took a bath in the holy river and changed his dress to saffron clothes. Like a hermit who practiced renunciation, he left all his worldly things and walked towards the Metropolitan city.

"Caw....! Caw....!" Hearing the cry of a crow, the crematorium operator woke up from his sleep. He was sweating all over and he cursed the nightmare. In the dim light, he noticed a young crow hopping out of the kiln. Other black crows on the tree were inviting the young one to join their company.

"It might have fallen down from the tree!" He thought.

He wished to help the young crow join the other black crows on the tree. But seeing the crematorium operator, the frightened young crow once again hopped into the kiln. A lightning passed through his heart. He should rescue the poor young crow! He walked into the kiln and the young crow was hopping towards the dead body. The young crow cried, "Caw...!" and, in order to make it friendly with him, he imitated its voice and cried "Caw....!"

Suddenly, the power supply returned and the automatic door of the kiln closed with a 'click' sound. No more cries from the black crows; they might have peacefully settled on the tree!

Author's Note: There is a superstition in India that black crows are the souls of the dead. On death anniversaries of dear relatives, people used to give food to these crows.

29

AFTER THE LAST DINNER

My last dinner was a sumptuous one!

As you know, we Malayalees or the people of Kerala in South India had no custom of taking supper, but only 'meals', a local usage meaning dinner, and if one should give names, they could be named as 'morning meals', 'noon meals', 'evening meals' or 'night meals', and we considered 'supper' only as something European.

And it was really a heavy dinner! It was 'heavy' because for the past few months I had been avoiding heavy meals, especially 'night meals', following my doctor's advice. They caused me some sort of muscular pain or, at times, gastric uneasiness. But how long one could depend on light food 'diet', irrespective of the fact that one suffered from ailments related to liver, kidney and heart?

To cut the tale short, I could not resist my temptation when I sat before a sumptuous dinner. I heartily took the delicious items one after another and went to sleep, after performing my regular prayers with the usual calisthenics involved in it.

Perhaps, I was in sound sleep, for I could keep only a vague memory of what happened to me during that night. It all started with a sweating of the body, with an increase in the weight of my body and a slight shortage of oxygen in the breathing air. I wished to wipe away the sweat off my forehead but I felt my hands too heavy to do so. Two or three times I took deep breaths and, then, all of a sudden, I felt completely relaxed.

No more was I sweating; a sort of chillness overwhelmed me as if I were anointed by some mint-oil. Neither was there any breathing problem nor the feeling of heaviness. I became so light that I found myself slowly moving up and up like a hydrogen balloon!

Just before my face touched the roof of my room, I quickly turned down only to see for a second my body lying motionless on the bed. Soon I was above my house, and I moved up and up and up like a tress of mist or a piece of cloud flying in the wind.

It was really a wonderful experience, as if you were an astronaut. Perhaps Yuri Gagarin or Neil Armstrong might have enjoyed such sights. I saw a myriad of planets and stars glittering around me against a light turquoise-blue sky. A strange but sweet silence prevailed everywhere.

Soon the stars and planets disappeared and I continued my flying towards a large rainbow arch. Some unwitting sensation reminded me that I was nearing to heaven's entrance! Unlike what they preached on earth, it was a large place with a large gate! The whole place was covered with thick cloud and I could see nothing but the gate.

Through the cleft of the doors, I tried to see what was inside or what trees were growing there, whether the kalpavriksha, the apple-tree or the date-palm, or at least, what the Heavenly color was, whether saffron, white or green as the Hindus, the Christians and the Muslims respectively believe. But everything was vague and misty.

Through the slight opening between the doors, chillness strained out and I felt as if one felt on earth while walking outside the open-door of a fully air-conditioned textile shop on a very hot day!

On the rainbow, the name of the place was written in a strange language and, so, I met the old gate-keeper and asked him: "Oh, Holy Grandfather! Is it Heaven? I can't read the inscription on the arch!"

Of course, I was sure that I would go only to heaven because a just God could never give two punishments to a person for the same crime. And my only crime was that I lived like a human being, for which I suffered a hellish life on earth itself.

"Yes! This is Heaven," the gate-keeper replied. After a moment, he continued, as if he understood my thoughts: "The inscription on the arch is in a language that existed before the construction of the Tower of Babel, the only language known both to God and Man!"

Of course, that language was extinct from the earth, I thought. Soon I realized why modern human beings failed to understand the words of God! But does it also mean that all the prayers made by human beings in different languages were not understood by God? I wondered.

I doubtfully looked into the eyes of the old gate-keeper. Suddenly I sensed the smell of fish and I understood that the gate-keeper of heaven was none but the Big Fisherman! I kissed his hand, in the earthly fashion, and said in a pleading voice: "Oh, Holy Grandpa, before I enter into Heaven, will you please kindly allow me to see Hell?"

I heard that there was a gulf in between Heaven and Hell and that once you entered it, it would be impossible to visit the other place. And before my entrance to Heaven, I wished to make a triumphant show-off to my dear relatives and friends who had made my earthly life a miserable hell!

The Holy Pope-Patriarch-Catholicos nodded his head and pointed his forefinger to the left of the rainbow gate. I moved by the left side of the rainbow arch and floated towards a smaller arch. At the gate, a scantily bearded man in his black gown greeted me. He had the profile of a bishop whom I knew on earth! With great surprise, I asked him: "Oh, Holy Father! How did you happen to be here?"

With sadness in his tone, he said: "You see! I am a sinner of vanity, favoritism and credulousness. I committed a small sin for which I have to stay here for a while. After that, I will also join you in Heaven!"

There was a tone of extreme sadness in his voice. He continued: "Of course, we bishops show our sheep the way to heaven. We are like wayside pointers which never go to the destination mentioned on them."

I kissed his hand in the earthly fashion and he seemed to be very happy about it. I looked around and found it like a deserted place unlike what they preached.

"Is it really Hell?" I asked with surprise, for I expected a larger crowd there.

"Yes! This is Hell," he replied. After a while, he continued: "Usually priests and religious leaders of all religions and cults of the world who cheat their fellow human beings in the name of God are admitted here. Of course, those who try to snatch 'the kingdom, the power and the glory' and keep it for themselves in the name of God are given preference."

The whole place was under a thick fire and the doors were tightly closed. So I said in pleading voice: "Oh, Holy Father! Will you please allow me to see my dear relatives and friends who suffer inside?"

"No!" He cried: "You're destined for Heaven and, so, you can't enter Hell! Now, leave this place! See, I am very busy, and it's time for my prayer!"

I tried to recollect those words and that darkened face from my earthly experience somewhere in a Bishop's Palace! I muttered: "Incorrigible!"

Even on earth, my wishes were never fulfilled, I thought. Before I entered Heaven, I wished to have a last look at those people who created Hell for me on earth. I was in a dilemma!

Soon a host of angels came towards me from the direction of Heaven. They had the faces of my dear relatives and friends! In fact, I had forgotten the magic of mass salvation! They pulled at me and drew me up towards Heaven. On the way, I heard the familiar voice of my wife, with the usual complaining tone, from my left side: "Why do you linger around Hell! Your place is in Heaven and we were all waiting for you there!"

You knew what happened to me later! I realized that God could also give two punishments to a person for the same crime! And I too was in Heaven! Then my only prayer was: "Thy will be done in heaven as it is on earth! Amen!"

CONFESSIONS OF A WRITER

Prof. Dr. V. Alexander Raju M.A., Ph.D., LL.B.

Writing creative literature is not exactly a deliberate act of a true writer, and even if one labors to do so, it will not take birth from one's travail alone. It is an act of compulsion either from 'above' or beyond normal instincts, or of a divine mission self-realized by selected individuals. Such persons cannot live without writing, and this phenomenon occurs to them, perhaps, due to some disassociation of the veins or dislocation of neurons in the brain, as some biologists might say, or to certain guidance of some supernatural powers as the spiritualists might say.

It is mandatory for the persons concerned, as if it is in the case of pregnant women to deliver; sometimes matured babies, sometimes premature ones, other times dead ones or even abortions at the fetus stage are also possible. It is like the eviction of an itching thorn stuck into one's body that, if not pushed out or taken out naturally, may lead to some cancerous growth, culminating into a greater disaster or to some sort of contamination of the whole body. Fortunately or otherwise, I too became a victim to that rare phenomenon that I cannot help but writing.

Whatever the influence may be, human beings sing, tell or write from time immemorial, beyond the times of Vyasa, Valmiki and Homer, and still continue to do so. Some of their productions influenced even the very entity of human civilizations by controlling the physical, emotional, spiritual and social existence of individuals in society. Sometimes, my writings may not be of any benefit for the world, neither for my country nor for my friends and relatives, but it has been giving peace and solace to my disturbed mind, a kind of private or selfish relief. And that is the only answer to the question why I write.

Secondly, some of my readers ask me, especially after the publication of my second collection of poems, *Sprouts of Indignation*, why I write about the evils of society, political, religious and social anomalies with which the world otherwise has been accustomed to. Personally I believe that it is the duty of a writer to scan the surroundings in which he lives and highlight the maladies of the age and, thereby, give an opportunity for the society to correct itself, immediately or in the near future, so that it can attain a better position in which individuals can enjoy freedom without curtailing the rights of others. In the natural course, it may take much more time, so that many generations remain unlucky to attain that stage, if not rectified earlier, as their 'clear stream of reason' loses its way into 'the dreary desert sands of dead habit'. Changes are inevitable, historically and sociologically, and a writer's duty is to sow the seeds of a social revolution.

Writers must be optimistic while sowing the seeds of social change and they should not feel either exhausted of sowing or disappointed at the fruitlessness of their labor. As it is explained by Jesus in his parable of the Sower and the Seeds, some seeds may fall by the wayside, some on stony places, some among thorns and some "into good ground and bring forth fruit, some an hundredfold, some sixtyfold, some thirtyfold!" Remember that even those seeds that fall on the fertile soil fail to give equal amount of harvest, 'some thirty times, some sixty times and some others hundred times'! Let me add one more type of seed that Jesus forgot in the parable; some seeds may lie dormant in the fertile soil, perhaps, for years and years, awaiting the right moment for their germination.

A seed is a seed and an idea is an idea; they never go to waste or remain unaware. Sometime, somewhere, someone will be benefited by them, and the sower may not be alive to see them grow and give harvest. Of course, in a sort of spasmodic seizure of confidence, I tried to save my fellow human beings from their passive acceptance of the generality of a culture into which they adjust their existence, always feigning to feel proud of it by clinging hypocritically to the notion that everything is good with this world. I appreciate their confidence because I know that a lack of optimism is the last straw that breaks the camel's back! But if I cannot show them the way, some others will definitely do so, and my birth may turn to be mere waste. Remember what our Indian sages say: "Do your duty and do not flirt with the fruits of it." I tried to do my duty in the best possible manner, and that is my answer to the second question.

Once some of my student-friends asked me why I write in English and why not in my mother tongue. Well, we all have our different mother tongues and we use them like honeybees use their own natural and instinctive language, a sort of rudimentary form of communication for their mechanical and mindless association within a well-disciplined society. But for human beings, as they are rational creatures, they get their language as an acquired skill, and the instinctive language in them can be used generally for crying, begging or praising their gods and goddesses, and specifically for acquiring language skills. So I insist the study of a universal tongue for every elite and farsighted human being, excepting those brute majorities of people with limited or inverted vision of life, who are either less ambitious or fully satisfied or well-adjusted with the limitations of their life under native surroundings.

As language is not inherent in man, except for the capacity for language, unlike the honeybees, it becomes mandatory for him to learn it, like many other skills needed for existence, especially in a world which has been shrinking into a global village, where the limitations of the local tongue fail to facilitate the affairs and transactions of a global society. Of course, in closely-knit societies, in the past, the importance of language is seen in pristine clarity, and still we use it exclusively for praising our gods and goddesses. I write in English for the simple reason that I am incapable of writing literature in my mother tongue which I use usually for my day-to-day silly and frivolous talks, homely interactions, formal conversations and for discussing or writing about regional issues which have no wider scope.

When I was teaching the following lines from a poem written by the Indian poetess Kamala Das, 'I speak in three languages, write in two and dream in one', many of my students were tempted to think in an ordinary manner that the poetess dreams in her mother tongue which, of course, is similar to say that the British infants make their first cry in English and the North Indian infants in Hindi and the Keralite-infants in Malayalam. In fact, the language in which one dreams is common to all living human beings all over the world and this language works in every individual brain just like the language of the computer, the 'off and on' language of electricity, the power by which our heart starts and continues its beating, and produces results depending only on the materials fed to it.

However, I write in my mother tongue too when the scope of the subject is too limited to local environment, and other times, in English, as the materials fed into my brain have a considerable dominance over the other. You spontaneously talk or write in a language of which the materials, in the form of vocabulary and language skills, ideas and emotions, intellectual, physical, emotional and spiritual experiences as well as a myriad of other ingredients needed for a writer are deliberately and naturally fed into your brain. Of course, it is the living circumstances that help you in acquiring these materials, and those who are less fortunate shall not feel jealousy of others who are blessed with more opportunities in life.

In the past, all societies, smaller or larger, held the notion that only their language is divine and its spirit cannot be translated into other languages due to the potency of the words and phrases in it, as in the case of the holy book in Arabic, the Koran. Many of my friends who write excellently in their vernacular claim that they could write effectively in their mother tongue, and they confess that whenever they try in English or in any other second language, their literature lacks its real spirit. Of course, it is natural that any writer in any language should feel the presence or absence of that so-called 'spirit', especially in the process of the self-assessment of his work, and an ingenuous writer can easily feel the difference or variation in his own different works. "African societies in the past held similar notions about language and the potency of words," says Chinua Achebe, and many of us still, even in the twenty first century, remain slaves to such biased ideas.

I am not against the growth of vernacular literature, and I am always for it; but the vernacular writers shall not try to survive at the cost of a universal language and literature by getting applause of the natives or regionalists through cheap gimmicks. If I use terms suggested by the psychologist Charles Spearmann, I must say that some of our writers with much developed S-factor of intelligence, join hands with others with mere G-factor of intelligence in making a fuss about English.

It is unfortunate that some of our regional writers' parochialism has too much politics in it that they should listen to the warning given by George Orwell in his *Politics and the English Language* that language can be used not only for expressing thought but for concealing thought or even preventing thought and abstain from unhealthy provocations. Or are we not still fully relieved from the inferiority complex that forced us once to hate what all belong to the British, our one time masters, and recovered completely from the traumatic effects of their colonization, so that we can think of them and their legacy to the world on equal terms?

There is a foolish notion even among certain critics that bilingual writers first think in their mother tongue and then write in a second language that their writing loses the natural flavor. In fact, all languages are second if there is a language for thinking and, if so, every piece of writing is at least once removed from the original and, therefore, every writing is a trans-creation. Human beings all over the world think in the same language which is instinctive, though its realization varies in accordance with the individual. Therefore, whether a person writes in his mother tongue or in a second language or even in a third, fourth or fifth language has nothing to do with the process of creativity which cannot be a translation as some of our critics and writers think.

Or perhaps, there is another reason for their misunderstanding and, I think, the following explanation will be sufficient to expose their misunderstanding. A translation is always a reproduction in a second language, an approximation of the original done in another language. No monolingual writer is happy with the translations of his works done even by professional translators or trans-creative writers with mastery over the two languages and thorough comprehension of the subject matter to be rendered. A major problem faced by a translator is the nature of the text to be translated, both the nature of the content to be rendered and the nature of the language this content is couched in. His problem is further complicated in the case of fictional and creative works, as some specific elements in the original are wholly untranslatable to any other language.

A creative writer thinks only in his language cultural context while his English translator has to think in the English language cultural context. A good creative writer infuses in his works cultural values as well as the vision and views of the people of a particular time and place as reflected in the thoughts, beliefs and actions of some selected characters. But some of these elements in the original work could hardly be expected to have, let alone exact correspondents, even similar ones, in the English language cultural context. Therefore, the translator seeks and finds his own way of tackling or coping with this problem, by giving at least an inkling of what the original text intends to convey. Perhaps, an approximation which is justifiable should be appreciated. But the writer of the original work is never fully satisfied and he is tempted to think scrupulously that all writings in a second language are mere approximations. Of course I admit that while writing in English, I faced problems related to idiomatic expressions, phrases, proverbs and sayings, due to the lack of my familiarity with them.

The phrase 'Indian Literature' has a much wider meaning that it will give you only a general idea. In a multi-lingual country like India, it means the total volume of literature produced in more than a score of regional languages, including the so-called 'Inglish'. To some conservatives, it means only those classics produced in the remote past, in that apparently dead, great language Sanskrit, and not the modern writings which for them are not up to the level of real literature.

Because of our blind national parochialism, if not linguistic fanaticism, we are tempted to vote for a particular regional literature and place it on the throne of national literature. But 'a national literature is one that takes the whole nation for its province and has a realized or potential audience throughout its territory', as Chinua Achebe pointed out. In other words, literature written in a language which is familiar to all the multilingual groups of the country can be accepted as the national literature of that country.

Here, I am not speaking about the formal declaration of a particular language as the national language of a particular nation. Any government can declare any language as the national language, with the brutish majority of its supporters or even with the casting vote of the Head of the Nation as it once happened in India, by making an amendment in the Constitution. The excuse might be that either more people speak that language compared to other major languages in the country, as in the case of India, or that language has comparatively more literary merit than other languages spoken by the majority of the people, as in the case of Ethiopia where Amharic is the national language even though more people speak Oromic. And I am proud of India's spirit of democracy that made her declare all languages in India as her national languages. In short, an actual national language is the language that can be understood by most of the people in the country who belong to different ethnic or linguistic groups.

In Ethiopia, where I served as a Professor of English for three years, there are about eighty ethnic groups and almost a similar number of languages, each language with a definite culture of its own. Though there is an effort to spread the Amharic language as a national language, there is no evidence of destroying other languages, unlike what the promoters of the Arab culture and language did in the past. Nobody can imagine the total number of small languages destroyed by the Arabs in their enthusiasm to spread their language which is an indispensable part of their religion. In Libya, some of my students complained that their mother tongue Berber was completely discouraged by the Arabic speaking majority. If this is the case in Libya where people enjoy more religious freedom than in any other Islamic countries, just imagine the number of languages all over the Arab World massacred in the name of Arabic!

There are many Indians who think of English as a 'foreign' language because England is a foreign country. They think on the basis of territory and ignore the fact that the relationship between a language and a country is quite remote. For example, Tigrenia is not a foreign language for Ethiopians though it is the national language of Eritrea and Chinese is a foreign language for Tibetans though Tibet is a part of China. Once, in an interview at Gangtok, Sikkim, I asked the then Indian Prime Minister Morarji Desai why he could not include the Nepali language in the 8th schedule of the Indian Constitution, and he replied that Nepali was a foreign language! He either did not know that Nepali is the mother tongue of more than 80% of the people in Sikkim, a State in India, or conveniently ignored that fact. Of course, Mrs. Indira Gandhi could do it within a year after Morarjibhai's funny prattle.

What I try to drive home is that any country may be made larger by annexing neighboring countries or made smaller by dividing it into smaller ones due to political or other reasons. When we talk about language, political boundaries are of least concern. We cannot ignore the historical fact that Great Britain had an empire 'where the sun never sets' and English was implemented or used as a lingua franca almost all over the world. Perhaps, the greatest contribution of Great Britain to the legacy of human civilization is that they gave an international tongue and, thereby, no longer made English a foreign language for the whole of humanity.

Once political boundaries are ignored, we come to language-boundaries and, then all languages, other than the mother tongue, appear 'foreign'. Then, what exactly is this so-called 'foreign'? It is as simple as that we Indians say of our foreign pants and shirt! In fact, they are foreign but without them we cannot live in the present age. Do you think that something foreign could never become native? Nepali, a foreign language, became an Indian language within the wink of an eye! Many people foolishly think that our culture, our religion and our language are only for us and no one else should be benefited by them, as we do not want to be benefited by the culture, religion and language of others! There are also people who think that their culture, religion and language should dominate the whole world by destroying all other cultures, religions and languages! But nobody can deny that every culture, religion and language is much benefited by the influence of other cultures, religions and languages. In fact, it was a sort of reciprocal give, take and share process and we must be proud of it.

As we all know, today's India is the arbitrary creation of the British. The British helped us to become a big political unit by uniting a number of scattered but autocephalous native states. It is quite strange that even in the twenty first century there are people in India who believe that India was a single political unit ruled by a single emperor, about three thousand years ago! It is natural that they are tempted to believe so by taking the literal meaning of the story presented in our great epics, the Ramayana and the Maha Bharatha. Of course, many of us could not think of anything else without bringing politics into it! Why can't we think that India in those ancient days was a single cultural unit, not a single political unit, and the influence of the great epics reached every nook and corner of India? Of course, ancient India was neither a single political unit, nor a single linguistic unit, as Sanskrit language could not enter into the core of Tamil language that was then dominating almost all parts of South India. It is taken for granted that a more or less similar culture, or an amalgamation of many religious cultures, is flowing through the veins of all Indians but there is no trace of truth when some people say that once we were a single nation , except in a figurative manner of our great epics.

English is a second language, and not a mother tongue, for the majority of Indians. When certain critics asked Chinua Achebe whether a person, after learning a second language, could write creative literature effectively in it, he replied affirmatively and said that we had enough examples of writers who had performed the feat of writing effectively in a second language and their books were proof enough that they could make even an imperfectly learnt second language do amazing things. If you ask me whether I can use English as smoothly as my mother tongue, I must say that I cannot, for one thing that I have many other personal uses with my mother tongue. For another matter, a mother tongue is only a daily use language, all those using it need not be writers in it, and, for many of them, the inspiration as well as the capacity and talent to write in it may not be so strong.

When we consider a mother tongue, it is natural that we think about it in a generalized manner and even carried away by the vast number of people who use it. In fact, every mother tongue has a pyramidal structure, once divided into two, the upper half is the perfect language and the lower half is the imperfect language. The perfect language is used, as it is the true or genuine language, for professional, academic, religious, official and literary purposes. The imperfect language is used, as it is the daily-use or corrupt language, for informal conversations, personal flirting and common prattling. A non-native speaker can never fully learn this imperfect language as it is full of slang usages, colloquial expressions, senseless vituperations and words or sounds which have only momentary meanings as well as a myriad of nuances. To learn a language means to learn the perfect language through academic efforts and not the imperfect part of it that can be learned only through one's physical presence among the native speakers. Any person who learned this perfect language could claim that he learned a language, and a person who learned the imperfect language could only say that he learned to converse with the natives. I remember a waiter in a restaurant in Gangtok who could speak about twenty three languages, including Chinese, but not a single one to write! It is unfortunate that we usually evaluate the merit of a language based on the number of people who use this imperfect language. Of course, fiction writers, like Vaikom Mohammed Basheer, used this imperfect or slang language of Malayalam for the realistic presentation of his characters, and certain non-native English writers who got the opportunity to live among the native speakers of English could also use the same effectively in their creative works.

Now, the question my friends generally ask is, "Can a non-native write effectively in English?" A more serious question they raise is, "Is it necessary for a non-native to write in English?" These questions were also asked to Chinua Achebe and his answers acquired a sort of perennial freshness. Of course many non-native English writers all over the world used to face similar situations. Should we Indians, categorized as Hindiwalla, Bengali, Malayalee, Tamilian, Kannadiga or Marathiwalla, leave our respective mother tongue and write in another's mother tongue? Is it not a self betrayal, betrayal of one's own language, culture and nationality? My answer is, "No! Never!" I never betrayed myself and I have no guilty conscience in writing in English, as I wrote in English due to genuine inspiration. I am, rather, really proud in presenting my culture and nationality through my writings in an international language before a large readership belonging to various races, cultures, religions, languages and nationalities. I must confess that it was my own mother tongue that betrayed me without giving genuine inspiration, and I do not know whether it was my mistake or the mistake of my mother tongue. Nevertheless, a vast majority of people who use my mother tongue for their daily use were incapable of getting the spiritual gift of inspiration. Of course, my environment was suitable for me to be inspired and to think and write in English. And there is always the presence of a divine power behind every writer whether he writes in his mother tongue or in a second language, especially in a foreign tongue that appears strange like an oracle to the laymen.

Of course, I began my creative writing first in my mother tongue, Malayalam, one of the leading modern languages in India. I had a tedious and exhausting childhood and I could realize my literary flame hidden under the ashes of harsh and monotonous daily routine only after leaving my secondary school. There are many people who nurture sweet memories about their childhood but I do not have any such foolish nostalgia; each new day from the stock of future gave me more thrill and enthusiasm than those days of the rotten past. It was on the previous night of our celebrated Onam day in 1967 that I wrote my first poem, of course, it was in Malayalam, my mother tongue. Though Onam is a harvest festival, the story behind it is quite unique. According to the legend, in the past, there was an ideal king called Mahabali who ruled our part of south India named Kerala or the Land of Coconut Trees.

During his reign, there were no crimes, no scarcity, no inequality, no injustice and no corruption so that his subjects lived in peace and happiness. Then came Vamana, an incarnation of Lord Mahavishnu, played a trick on the benevolent king and sent him down into the underworld, with a boon to come back once in a year to see his subjects. Despite our misery and vices, on the day of Onam we pretend to be good and happy just to please our ideal king who is believed to visit us on that day! My poem was about the joy and cheerfulness of the festival and about the dream of a world of peace and prosperity, a world of equality, fraternity and liberty, a world free from war, corruption and starvation, maybe a Utopian idea but without such a dream how could we live in this world?

After the Onam holidays, I returned to my college. One day my friend and classmate one Mr. Divakaran showed me a letter sent by his eldest sister. He was in tears and I was anxious to know the reason. The letter described the miserable life of that girl who had to sacrifice her life, being treated like a milch-cow by her parents, for the up-bringing of her younger sisters and brothers. On that night, based on that letter, I wrote my first short story in my mother tongue, Malayalam. Since then, I have written dozens and scores of poems and stories, both in Malayalam and English; many of them never came to the limelight but I enjoyed myself reading them again and again.

My first book in Malayalam was a collection of ten short stories titled Belivediyile Thirikal (*Candles on the Altar*) published in 1985. Then I was a Sunday school teacher and my idea was to give moral messages to my students, presenting certain fictitious characters in the background of places familiar to me during 'my wanderings through the length and breadth of India'. Those were stories I wrote for the manuscript-magazine called 'Trumpet' brought out by the

Youth League in our church and, as its editor I had to find sufficient materials every month. My second book in Malayalam was a collection of fifteen short stories titled Adaminte Mukhangal (*Many Faces of Adam*) published by the Christian Literature Society, Tiruvalla, Kerala in 1991. During that period I had been writing my novel *Upon This Bank and Shoal*, the title I had given to it then was 'I am That I am', and when Rev. Dr. T. M. Philip, the Director of CLS, suggested the publication of a book, I immediately translated selected parts of the novel, made slight changes and handed over them to the publisher. All the one thousand copies of the book were sold out like hot cakes and CLS became the only publisher who compelled me to receive even the last penny of its royalty.

My preface to *Many Faces of Adam* was actually an introduction to my novel *Upon This Bank and Shoal*. I quote the last paragraph: Adam began his journey right into the midst of contradictions. The quest, that begins from the dark hog-track of the past progresses into the bright royal path of the future. He who got the right to select according to his discretion, and blessed with prudence, continued his journey from one place to another and from one thing to another... from evil to virtue, from grief to happiness, from ignorance to wisdom, from despair to hope, from the sword of revenge to the cross of sacrifice, from death to life... to eternal life... he continues his journey. I quote the above only to suggest the universality of the theme in the novel. I was really honored when Rev. Dr. K. M. George, then working with the World Council of Churches in Geneva, currently serving as the Principal of the Orthodox Theological Seminary at Kottayam, Kerala, wrote an appreciation of my stories in *Many Faces of Adam*. As his words are quite applicable even in the case of *Upon This Bank and Shoal*, I quote: Reading is interpretation. The amalgamation of the word and its meaning happens not in the text but in the mind of the reader. This material unity is interpretable. And there is no reading without interpretation. For instance, the word 'heaven' evokes a different sense of meaning to each different reader. Here, the horizon of meaning is determined on the basis of the formerly acquired culture, preconceptions and presuppositions of each reader. For the purpose of ordinary conversation, a general level of meaning is given to this word as well as to all words, but each word evokes a very different sense of meaning, a meaning beyond its casual meaning, to each individual and to each social group. This unique consciousness of meaning is what we call interpretation. And today Hermeneutics which analyses the complexity of interpretation has become a very vast area of study. Thanks to the critic, these words encouraged the readers of all my creative writings.

I learned my mother tongue as a second language till my graduation and this helped me to become a bilingual writer, at least, a writer of columns in certain periodicals. I began my career as a journalist and I learned to react on every current issue. This compelled me to write regular columns in newspapers and, as the lifespan of a news-daily is only a day, many pieces of my writings also disappeared together with those pulp-scraps. In 1977, immediately after the withdrawal of the most infamous Emergency in India, my first column captioned 'The Wanderer's Diary' appeared in *Sikkim Express*, a news-daily published from Gangtok, Sikkim. Of course, the idea of the Wanderer came from *The Haunted Man*, the novel which I was then writing. Two regular columns I wrote in Malayalam were Kashtam! Nham Enghottu? (Alas! Where do we go?) in a magazine called *Kamaladalam* and Mata-sauhardhathinte Vazhikal (The Ways of Ecumenism) in a quarterly named *Snehavani*. About fifty articles on social and political issues came in *Kamaladalam* and about twenty-five articles on religious faith came in *Snehavani*. I gratefully remember Dr. G. S. Balarama Gupta, the editor of *The Journal of Indian Writing in English*, who requested me to prepare critical write-ups on newly published books for his journal which helped me to develop talent as a critic.

In my acknowledgment for *The Haunted Man*, I clearly pointed out that it was my chance to take English Language and Literature as the subject for my degree studies, to read English books than what were given in the curriculum, to travel all over India where my mother tongue had no use at all and to get a job in a place like Sikkim where I had to use English as a second mother tongue that helped me to become a writer in English. Of course, in those days, when telephones were rare or calls were very expensive, I had to live for many months even without uttering a single word in my mother tongue. Let me quote: As a student of literature, I have always been drawn to the skits of Samuel Butler, Jonathan Swift, Thomas More and George Orwell. The vein and form of my novel, *The Haunted Man*, have been to a great extent derived from these renowned masters. Though books are 'bloodless substitutes,' I am extremely thankful to a myriad of writers and their works for making me what I am today. As Tennyson's Ulysses says, 'I am a part of all that I have met,' be it in the form of peoples, of places or of books. This novel (*The Haunted Man*) contains a number of quotes and thematic references to the past masters and contemporary quill-wielders. Many of these echoes have been plucked from my surrealistic memory and, hence, some of them cannot be properly acknowledged. Therefore, I hereby acknowledge my debt of gratitude to all those authors and their publishers from whose pages this novel has derived its sustenance.

I quote again from the acknowledgment: A decade of my wanderings through the length and width of India and my not too short sojourn in the Himalayan Valley gave me an everlasting mine of ideas and a continuous source of inspiration that would last a whole lifespan of a creative writer. Then I was so inquisitive, so idealistic, so enthusiastic and so sensitive that my life in those days was a buoyant experience of 'aching joys' and 'dizzy raptures'. With the exception of a few sentences or paragraphs which I revised or added to it later, this novel was almost wholly conceived and written in that hey-day of my existence. I feel quite satisfied in having been able to solidify that unforgettable past through my first novel, *The Haunted Man*.

The amalgamation of the dreamscape, the experience and the literaturescape is the backbone of my novel *The Haunted Man*. Many of us see dreams during our sound sleep and forget them sooner or later. Most of us enjoy reveries but they too leave our minds in the passage of days. Though what we are really is the sum-total of our experience, and we feel its value while using it in our talks or writings. Those moments of thrills we felt while reading books will remain dormant in us if we could not convey them to others through our writings. Many of those who dream or experience or read could not write, some of them write but their works are not published so that perish with their authors and a few of them write and publish so that their dreams, experiences and vast readings turn useful for others; they are solidified for posterity.

Creative writing, in a way, is the catharsis of the writer. Unpleasant social, political or religious situations hurt the heart of a writer and he cannot rest until such thorns are ejected from his heart. The political situation in India, existed in 1975, provoked me to write my novel *The Haunted Man*, even though its theme is universal. I quote from the brief note I wrote for the novel: Power corrupts and absolute power corrupts absolutely; this is true under dictatorship, totalitarianism and fundamentalism, and democracy as well. Slavery, bondage, suppression and discrimination follow when absolute power corrupts. Perhaps, an Abraham Lincoln could legally put an end to the physical slavery, but its manifestation in various other forms related to race, including color and caste, culture, language, religion, nationality and political system remains a threat to man's spirit of freedom. The nineteen month-long Emergency declared in India in 1975 would be a relatively insignificant event in the political history of the world's largest democracy. But, when *The Haunted Man*, allegorically presents the agony of the people, gasping for breath under its heavy yoke, the subject gains universality. Through dozens of symbolic episodes and references picked up from the world of literaturescape, the novel unravels the severity of such physical and psychological suppressions of the helpless masses and, thereby, not only creates awareness among freedom-loving peoples but also tenders a warning to the whole world.

I wrote, at first, for myself and that is why I was very late in publishing my writings. My first published work is a One Act Play titled *The Holy Land* which came out in the Baselius College Annual, 1972. Sparing six pages of the magazine for the work of a student was rare in those days but I consider it an honor given to me by the editorial board. Different parts of my novel *Upon This Bank and Shoal* appeared in various periodicals, either in English or as their Malayalam translation, even thirty years before it appeared in the book form in 2008! I remember, the Golden Jubilee Souvenir published in 1975 by my parish, the Nedumavu St. Paul's Orthodox Church, contained a small translated piece from the novel with the title '*Upputhoonukal*' or the Pillars of Salt. Another instance is the publication of the periodical, Stir the Fire, a Journal of Creative and Critical Writings in Indian English, which was the outcome of about thirty years of my waiting and contemplation. I reproduce below my editorial for its first edition, as it shows how the idea germinated in my heart about three and a half decades before:

"It was in the last week of March, 1974 that together with my friends, I climbed down the hill on which situates the University of Saugar, Sagar, Madhya Pradesh in India. Our M.A. final year examinations were successfully over and we had the idea to celebrate the event with a friend of ours who had been working as a military officer in the army camp down in the valley.

The evening sun was deep red when we set off to the camp. The twilight turned the hillside golden and, balancing ourselves on the small rocks and slippery pebbles that lay scattered, we trekked down through a deserted, narrow jungle path. Though it was a shortcut to the camp, both sides of the footpath were full of thorny bushes that often caught us at our shirts and pants and pulled us back as if giving a mute warning. Soon the sun set behind the hill and dusk began to cover the hillside with her dark blanket.

We managed to reach the valley only to find that our hog-track was blocked with barbed-wire fencing. Prasanna Babu, T.V. George, Thomas Muthalay, K.N. Many, K.R. Radhakrishnan, Somashekhara Karnavar and I stood there in utter bewilderment as the fence seemed endless on both ways.

We were all quite exhausted of walking down the hill-slope and as darkness was spreading fast, we listened to the suggestion made by Babu, the fattest member in our group. He pulled the barbed-wires sideways and made a space through which we could crawl through to the other side. Of course, Babu's shirt tore from top to bottom as he struggled through the fence. At last we all made it up and heaved hot sighs of relief.

It was quite dark and we walked forward cautiously for fear

of stepping on some poisonous jungle-snakes lurking under the dead leaves and dried twigs. Suddenly, our blood thickened in our veins, hearing a harsh stony voice, 'Dhammm…!' Two army sentinels were pointing their loaded guns against us and we stood frozen, though we did not know then that the word 'Dham' in Hindi meant 'halt' or 'don't move'!

They led us under gun-points towards their officer who told us that we would be prosecuted for trespassing into the prohibited military area. A tremor passed through us as he tried to console us saying, "Any way you're lucky! We used to shoot down, then and there, those spies who enter this compound!"

"We aren't spies but students, Sir!" I stammered, presenting my examination hall-ticket to him.

"But a crime is a crime and you know the dictum 'ignorantia juris ne excusate'," he said.

My friend Babu, once again suggested a new idea, of course, he had quite a stock of such stupid ideas, that we could return through the same space in the barbed-wire fence.

"Then, you will be punished twice, for crossing the fence two times!" cried the officer.

Our host in the camp came to know about this 'encroachment of spies', and he soon came to our rescue. The ordeal was only over when the officer said at last that he was only playing a farce; just to relieve him from the boredom of the army routine! He offered us a bottle of triple 'X' rum, the so-called 'horse-rum', which gave Indian military its legendary courage from the time of the British onwards!

It was midnight when the party was over and we walked all the way from the camp to our hostel along the main road. Neither the cold wind touched our body nor did the long walk affect our legs. In fact, we were floating along the road; the 'ghoda-rum' had that much booze! It seemed the most suitable occasion to think about our future which, of course, was quite uncertain and bleak for every Indian youth, and a wonderful idea germinated in my mind which I conveyed to my friend Many, the spelling of whose name was strange, of course: What about launching an English journal titled 'Stir the Fire?'

About three decades have passed since then, much water has flowed through the Ganges, and I feel proud of realizing that long cherished dream through the publication of my journal, 'Stir the Fire: A Journal of Creative and Critical Writing in Indian English'.

The above write-up came in the internet too, thanks to chowk.com. My idea is to disclose the fact that I began my creative writing even before 1970, my novel *The Haunted Man* in 1975, and *Upon This Bank and Shoal* even much earlier to this, perhaps, in 1972, though both the novels came to limelight about a quarter of a century later. This tempts me to say a few words about publishing what one has written. When you hear the dictum 'publish or perish', it is not merely an advertisement for the publisher but a universal truth that the unpublished works perish together with the author. I know quite a few writers of good poems and short stories, who were either reluctant to publish their works or not lucky enough to do so that their products of great and rare imagination disappeared from the face of the earth together with the creators. As Thomas Gray sang:

> Full many a germ of purest ray serene,
> The dark unfathomed caves of ocean bear,
> Full many a flower is to blush unseen
> And waste its sweetness on the desert air.

Only a few writers are lucky to get their works published. For many years, during my early days of writing, it was my habit to write poems or stories and enjoy myself by reading them several times. Though writing poems is comparatively an easier task, as it is spontaneous, requiring lesser technical strain, it gives the writer greater delight than other forms of literature. It is because, as the first Nobel Laureate from the Arab World, Naguib Mahfouz pointed out, 'Poetry is the result of sudden bursts of inspiration: a poet may receive the inspiration for a poem while sitting on a bus and be able to complete his poem as soon as he gets home'. But novels, short stories and plays need much toiling and a continuity of inspiration and, if not published, the writer should be blamed of being too selfish and cruel in utilizing his unique talent as well as his energy and time for his own pleasure.

There was also another reason that tempted me to publish my writings. In 1990, I faced an ordeal due to a tragedy that occurred in my career as a writer. From the rented house, we had moved to an old, small house and all our things that could not be adjusted in the rooms were dumped in a small cellar. All my manuscripts of poems, one-act plays, short stories and novels, the outcome of my ten years' toiling as a researcher, journalist and writer, from 1970 to 1979, were packed in a green canvas suitcase which was very strong and beautiful, made in China or Taiwan, and this was also kept with other things in that damp room. The most important among the manuscripts were my incomplete novels like *The Sobbing Souls of Ragas*, a social novel in which the pathetic life of the outcaste people in the New Christian Colony of Sagar in Madhya Pradesh, India, was presented, *The Nepal Palace*, a horror cum historical novel in which the story of the Rana (King) of Nepal who had to leave his country and settle down in Sagar, Madhya Pradesh, India, was described, *The Thirsty Ganges*, a social cum crime thriller in which the exploitation of the believers by the Pandas or the Brahmins at the Thriveni Sangam in Allahabad, Uttar Pradesh, India, was criticized and

A Twist in the Teesta, a political and historical novel in which the transition story of Sikkim and her history before and after it became a part of India was described. The suitcase also contained the unpublished Malayalam poems, stories and novels of my father as well as the letters he sent for me, in the care of my mother, when I was only a suckling infant, which I hoped to bring to life some time later. One day I took that suitcase to check a few documents in it and found that the whole contents had been changed into a block of mud; all my papers had turned food for a large kind of white termites!

The suitcase contained certain very important documents related to the novel *A Twist in the Teesta* such as a few 'top secret' files concerning the surrender of the Chogyal, the King of Sikkim, his edicts on Denzong, the escape of his wife, Hope Cook the Chogyalni, to the United States, the details of the Thengu rope-way and its Chinese connection, the accidental death of the Chogyal's son who was the heir to the throne, the banishment of the Kazi, Lhendup Dorji, and his return to Sikkim as the Chief Minister, the story of the Kazini Sahiba who had been a life-force behind the Kazi, the details of the early days of Chief Minister Nar Bahadur Bhandari's political growth as well as my interview with Morarji Desai, the then Prime Minister of India, and a lot of paper clippings cum unpublished articles about things that happened immediately after the joining of Sikkim with India. (I remember the Kazini Sahiba's hospitality when I and my senior journalist Mr. R. K. Singhal went to her house to express our condolence on the death of her pet dog 'Willy'; to be served with a few drinks of whisky by the hands of a Chief Minister's wife was unimaginable in India!) The most important document was a copy of Judge Basnet's book, *The Rape of Sikkim*, the original manuscript of it was confiscated by the secret police at the Bagdogra Airport while he was going to Calcutta to publish it during those days of the infamous Emergency Period in India. A lot of photographs I took and postcards with pictures which I collected from different historical places I visited during those days and old photographs of the golden age of the Rana of Nepal (then residing in Sagar, Madya Pradesh) and his royal family's pomp and glory during the time of the British Raj, which the Rana gave me as gifts were also lost in that mishap. The termites had eaten even the canvas pillow which I used during my travels and what left with me was the shell, just the outer covering of the suitcase! Then it was a long period of 'convalesce' that I passed by fondling whatever writings lucky enough to survive that catastrophe!

When my novel *The Haunted Man* came to the limelight with the help of Mr. N.N. Lalu, a former student of mine, some of my friends asked me why my writings carried criticisms against the political, religious or cultural conditions prevailing in the country. As a witness of the Emergency Period in India, I had to write that novel with certain obvious biased comments. Though similar comments can be traced in my collection of poems titled *Sprouts of Indignation (2003)*, they were spontaneous and, perhaps, the outcome of a sensitive mind or a habit. But if the question is 'why do you write', the answer given by T.S. Eliot is more than sufficient: You write because you feel the need to free yourself of something. And I believe that nobody could give a better definition to poetry than Dr. Samuel Johnson who said, "Poetry is the art of uniting pleasure with truth by calling imagination to the help of reason."

A paragraph from my preface to *Sprouts of Indignation* would make my point clear, and I quote: Man is a social animal and, therefore, no social being can ignore the unhealthy trends of power politics of our times. It is natural that every committed citizen is sensitive to what happens in and around him. Some put the matter for general discussion; others make harangues. But once a poet conceives an idea or absorbs a subject or develops an emotion, it continues to disturb his equanimity, pricking his conscience and piercing his body, mind and soul, and until he is relieved of that irritating thorn, he will remain quite restless. When a poem is composed, and delivered after an agonizing travail, he feels relieved of a heavy burden, and enjoys the real pleasure of relaxation, of course, only to be disturbed by another subject, idea or emotion. I used to have such ordeals and pleasures and I see many a bramble and briar on my way.

My humble desire was to become a mentor of society, and my writings display those efforts of mentoring. This corrective approach is more or less innate and it is well expressed in the blurb for my poetic debut, *Ripples and Pebbles (1989)*, I quote: It is an unusual collection of poems written over many years which sardonically portray the situation in contemporary India. Rather than 'Songs of Innocence', they are his 'Songs of Experience'. Flipping through the pages of this book, you will not fail to notice some poems of despair – despair about oppression, guilt, corruption, exploitation and squalor all around. If pessimism, cynicism and irony are the persistent notes of many of these poems, the mistake is not in the poet, but in the things he sees, hears and experiences around him.

When I discovered that writing poems is the best way to get relief from the tension you suffer from an uneven society, it was a consolation and I wrote poems to purify my soul. In fact, every poem I wrote resulted in the writer's catharsis, giving me a healthy relief. Of course, from time immemorial, human beings compose or write, sing or read and enjoy poetry. It is because the poet as well as the listener or reader feels more or less a similar thrill or pleasure while engaging in this strange, or rather spiritual, activity into which our body, mind and soul are equally involved.

When I wrote the preface for my third collection of poems, *Magic Chasm* (2007), I made this idea about writing poems clear in it. Let me reproduce a few paragraphs from it as they well-explain my point, I quote: A true poet is always sensitive to every wave of change that occurs in and around him and creatively reacts to it through the language of his heart, considering it a part of his life's mission. Once an idea is conceived, he becomes quite restless and, of course, he cannot help himself from falling unknowingly into this helpless predicament. His agony continues until he relieves himself of that thorn from his mind by writing it down in the form of a poem or any other form as the case may be. Thereby he cures himself, and the society at large, of the maladies which seem to him quite harmful to the ideal world he envisages. Thus he serves the world and makes his life worthy of living.

Poems are born, usually, all of a sudden like bolts from the clear blue. I believe in such 'heaven-sent moments' that kindle my consciousness to unexpected revelations that inspire and force me to compose and write down creative pieces. During such evanescent occasions, I used to feel as if I were struck by some sort of lightning and dazzling flash of it sends a sort of electric thrill through my body, mind and soul. Then I used to become a stranger to myself, or a mere tool in the possession of that divine power. This stirring of the fire, I believe, helps a human being to bring out the inherent talents, whether in sciences, arts or humanities including literature. It is a fact that the majority of human beings are unaware of the existence of this supernatural power hidden in them. This fire in their very being remains covered by the ashes of ignorance or laziness, or suppressed by the heavy burden of their usual day-to-day selfish activities. Once a person is liberated from the yoke of his ignorance or selfishness, by chance or deliberate efforts through meditation or hard-work, miracles happen, and no force on earth could extinguish the flames of fire thus stirred in him. In such persons, the power of this stirred fire helps to bring unexpected and surprising results which turn them worthy of living their human life in various ways that we generally term 'greatness'.

In short, poetry is the deliberate reaction of a sensitive human brain towards exciting experiences, perfected by acquired knowledge and conscious efforts. It is deliberate because it is the poetic outcome of a spontaneous or non-spontaneous individual exercise. The mental, emotional and spiritual temperament of a person is highly counted here. The reaction can be on anything or everything, let it be in the form of real experiences, ideas, events, thoughts, feelings and/or fancies, specifically or generally related both to individual and social subject matters. Acquired knowledge includes all kinds of experiences gained through imaginative thinking, sensual feeling and intellectual learning. Everybody cannot write poems, nor appreciate them, unless they possess a sensitive and responsive brain. But it is the hard work of a patient, courageous and duty-conscious poet that magnifies his instinctive talents and perfects his artistic product. And, of course, a good short story is like a good poem; the travail of the writer is more or less the same.

However, many arguments can be raised when we try to evaluate poems on the basis of the relevance of a poet's themes or the accuracy of his style or the appropriateness of his technique. Can an Indian poet ever ignore the instinctive surges of philosophy, morality, philanthropy, spirituality or even the so-called romantic tendencies of the eighteenth century while giving vent to his disturbing poetic inspiration? Don't you feel that the Indian poets are always sensitive to and haunted by these traits of emotions at the cost of disregarding the fact that the world has changed much and practically gone far ahead everywhere except in India? How can we blame them when they are too didactic or too rashly and clumsily sentimental? Is it not quite natural that a poet with deep concern for the world in which he lives, who is sensitive to various issues that haunt his fellow beings among whom he lives, always find the bleak and grim realities in everyday life? Though these controversial points remain unanswered, can they set aside the basic aspirations of 'homo sapiens' which may survive as long as the species exist on this planet? That is the reason why we see such romantic ingredients crowding in our poems and stories. However, such features turn to rainbows or gems and jewels in the hands of matured poets and we tolerate the poets and love their poems. We feel thrilled when we realize the charm and magic of the basic human passions inherent in such poems.

The language of poetry, or of literature at large, is the language of thrills. The word language should not be narrowed down to the syntax, diction or style. It includes all other effects of the elements of literature like the theme, the plot, the character, the technique and so on. In other words, any language empowered by literary elements and that is capable of giving thrills to the reader or listener is literary language. Our appreciation of literature, or any form of art in this respect, depends on the varying effects of the thrills passing through the person concerned. Of course, the power of these thrills varies in accordance with the mental or physical qualities of the individual concerned. Though many other ingredients can be pointed out for the success of the literary language, the ability to give thrills is inevitable for it.

The value of a poem, or of any other piece of literature, art, music or painting as the case may be, shall be assessed on the basis of the effect it creates in the reader, listener or observer. In the case of poetry, especially, the impact of such effects differs, depending on the reader concerned, so that it is quite difficult to measure it exactly. This effect also varies from 'thrills', thrills which are even too delicate that they pass through us unnoticed or remain within us for a long time without any visible influence in our life, to heavy 'shocks', shocks which at times are even unbearable to the ordinary hearts. It should be noted that many of us could feel only the shocks and not the delicate thrills, but through regular and deliberate practice all sensible and sensitive persons can train themselves to experience even the very light caresses of such heavenly waves.

These thrills or shocks are not merely physical but emotional and physiological as well. They are spontaneous and natural so that every human being experiences it but many of us are unaware of their immediate reaction within us delaying our usual response to them. These thrills and shocks stir our soul, rejuvenate our body, inspire our mind and instigate our every day-to-day activity, physical or mental. They work in us either with immediate effect or lie dormant for an appropriate moment for its activation. Of course, even our instinctive physical responses like sneezing, yawning, coughing, scratching, blinking and so on give a similar sort of thrill which are quite obvious to many of us. If a poem can evoke at least a tiny wavelet of a thrill, that piece undoubtedly has it own literary merits.

According to T.S. Eliot, the greatness of a poem lies not in the poet's personality reflected in it, not in its being interesting, not even in its profound content but it is the poet's detached expression of passions other than his own that contributes to the greatness of his work. Explaining this theory of impersonality in his *Tradition and Individual Talent*, Eliot presents the famous platinum analogy, equating the poetic process to a chemical reaction, and shows the true relation of the poem to the poet. When a bit of platinum is introduced into a chamber containing oxygen and sulfur dioxide, the two gases combine to form sulfurous acid (HSO4) which is an entirely new product. The combination takes place only in the presence of platinum that serves only as a catalyst, but the new product contains no trace of platinum. It must be noted that the bit of platinum used in the process does not undergo any change; it remains inert, neutral and unchanged.

The poet or the writer, of course, is an inevitable catalyst, with all his natural talents and spirit of response, his intelligence, skills and knowledge as well as his experience and sensitiveness. His thoughts and desires as well as his emotions and feelings are the materials that change into a new product, a poem or any other piece of art as the case may be. However, as Eliot points out, 'the more perfect the artist, the more completely separate in him will be the man who suffers and the mind that creates'. Therefore, if the poet is impersonal, the style of language also becomes immaterial as the greatness of a poem depends only on its effect in the reader or in its capability of giving thrills to the reader.

Some of my critics point out the autobiographical elements in my novels, especially in *Upon This Bank and Shoal*. Of course, when stories are written, one cannot avoid such things. Every novelist, knowingly or unknowingly, adds the spice of personal elements in his works to show fidelity to the subject matter or characters in them. After seeing one of my paintings, captioned *The Raped Forest*, in which trees are presented as nude women, a professor-cum-priest asked me who the model was! Of course, it was just a colleague's joke, but his idea was to laugh at my wife whom I might have accepted as a model if she had been willing! Those readers who know me personally try to link the events or characters in my novels to personal life. I can only laugh at their ignorance or pettiness!

However, if fiction is the outcome of a writer's exclusive

imagination, naturally his imagination is part of his autobiography. And I quote the lines: Oysters are we poets, said I, / With our life's essence make we pearls, / Bearing pain as they our flesh pierce, / Patiently the burden we suffer, / Brightening them with sap of joy, / That others enjoy ornamenting! Again I quote: Silk-worms, we poets, I resume, / Gormandize on mulberry leaves, / Often our own life sacrificed, / On the altar of others' delight, / And make precious silk with our life, / The product of our entity! (*Magic Chasm*, p.22) Well! This is my answer to the critics.

The style of language changes in accordance with the passage of time but the enjoying of a poem remains the same with every human being. In other words, the media change time to time, but the pleasure offered by art and literature remains the same. Though the experience of such thrills is similar to all, the outward expression of the experience varies in accordance with the familiarized habits of psychological reaction of the individual concerned and, naturally, we think that some persons enjoy such thrills more profoundly than others. It is evident from the history of literary language that the old flowery, pompous language is no longer giving delight to the reader. This shows that it is necessary for the poet to give more concern to his language than to the electric effect or thrill supplied by his new product. No artist can deliberately give this quality to his work as it is instinctive and spontaneous and depends on the reader or spectator concerned. In short, unless the reader gets proper training in appreciating art and literature scientifically, even though he can feel the thrills quite unaware, the real thrills he cannot realize or recognize while he is on this side of the grave and to him 'a thing of beauty' will never be 'a joy forever'.

We cannot ignore the fact that those who learn a language as a non-native speaker, or as a second language learner, always experience a particular drawback as writers. They cannot recognize the unique and minute nuances of music innate in every language. That is why many of our Indian English poets and their readers fail to feel the music of English poetry. In fact, a vast majority of people are incapable of fully enjoying the poems written even in their mother tongue! Yet we cannot forget that almost all our poets are successful in universalizing their personal experiences through their poems and this, undoubtedly, is the main quality that helps poetry survive the test of time. And I am sure that the creative and optimistic attitude of our poets will make this genre lively and lovely.

It is not merely the case of poets; other creative writers too face similar problems. The novel *Upon This Bank and Shoal* was a humble missionary effort on my part to unite legacy and destiny. It was the result of my quest for a link among past, present and future, an attempt to understand who we are, where we have come from and where we are going to. I began my writing with a sense of clear purpose and belonging, and the doors of possibilities were wide-open for me. Of course, we all start with our given heritage of family, congregation, society, place and time and we all build on it in ways that may be surprising or altogether new. Such a new way is evident in my first novel *The Haunted Man* in which the dreamscapes you find were the outcome of perceived life experiences, mostly recollected from my flights on the viewless wings of fancy. Man is basically a discoverer and an inventor, and if he is not ready to take up risky adventures, he will stand only at the port where he must embark upon. Social stigmas, especially religious ones, try to tie us to the harbor, but one has to release oneself from their knots and take a path 'less traveled by' which makes 'all the difference', as Robert Frost says, though it is suicidal to a certain extent to do so.

My friends, after reading the manuscript of *Upon This Bank and Shoal*, commented that certain thoughts, feelings and events presented in it are quite incongruous. Of course, in the fourth part of the novel, this incongruity is deliberately infused to show the senility of the protagonist. But we should not forget the fact that, even in our daily life, every human being has that peculiar proclivity to synthesize apparently incongruous thoughts, feelings and events. And we have our own individual voice too for such strange affiliations and or synthesis. My voice in the novel springs from my own cultural and perceived life experiences, including the agony or rapture offered by the blessed moments of imagination.

Another friend commented in an applauding tone that he was all for the subversion in it! In fact, there is nothing subversive in my work and I personally dislike all deliberate attempts of that sort in genuine writing. However, in certain situations, when a writer's freedom of expression is thwarted by the domination of popularly accepted religious or political ideologies and practices, his creativity may force him to present his thoughts in an exclusive manner which cannot be easily defined or termed as subversive. Then it is natural that a biased reader misunderstands the writer's conceiving and growth of the subject matter as well as the outcome in a language ingenious or esoteric as an oracle which can be compared only to the equivocal uttering of the three witches in *Macbeth* or the vague predictions of Nostradamus. As the mind of such a reader is contaminated with stagnant notions about good and evil, he could recognize, from a given text, only those meanings easy for him and all other aspects of the text are looked down upon by him with his limited, negative way of approach. In other words, whatever he believes to be 'fair' need not be 'fair' but 'foul' so that the result of his reaction is like that of the weird sisters: Fair is foul and foul is fair!

The term subversion is tentative; for a writer, every work is super-version! Many religious believers, who could not prove their faith rationally, coined the word 'heresy' to suppress everything that supposedly challenged their blind convictions. Thus those who could not appreciate a work of art as a work of art used to declare it subversion or heresy; or certain publishers did so just for the popularity of their products. Today, our religious beliefs are so strong and blind that books like *The Last Temptation of Christ* or *Satanic Verses* could hardly make any impact on the believers. Those believers who take up the protection of God as a duty for themselves are in fools' paradise! Let God the omnipotent, the omniscient and the omnipresent be our protector! It is the wobblers who are afraid of the so-called heresy or subversion and, thereby, turn into criminal extremists! Even God would be ashamed of a system where politicians and fundamentalists decide the merits of a literary work!

It is natural that the believers of an existing 'fantasy' will not allow any other fantasies to supersede or dominate over their beliefs or allow any sort of infringement on their rights and privileges. Good stories must be read on a symbolic level as they can be a vehicle for meanings that are the construction of the reader but a non-aesthetic reader, especially if he is a blind religious believer, fails to appreciate such works. When Naguib Mahfouz, the first Nobel Laureate from the Arab world, brought out his *Children of the Alley*, the Egyptian fundamentalists attacked him for a silly reason. When Arafa, a character in the novel, comes to know that Gabalawi has died and that all his learning is of no avail without the principles of his dead master, he calls for his resurrection, though he had never died or resurrected in the story, and this scene infuriated the so-called protectors of God, grouped under Al Azhar! My strong opinion is that man's imagination and its creative outcome is the only strong basis of every religion; man can enhance it by adding more to it either affirmatively or negatively. Neither could Dan Brown's *Da Vinci Code* nor Tazleema's *Lajja* harm a religion that has survived the test of time! In Hindu religion, both good and evil are the two faces of the same deity and the Semitic religions failed to understand the greatness of this philosophy; although certain modern Hindu cults, unfortunately, have recently begun to follow the latter's parochial line of thinking!

A superfluous reader of *Upon This Bank and Shoal* may suddenly jump to the conclusion that it is a theological novel. In fact, it deals with the perennial theme of man-woman relationship in a unique manner. Even in the twenty first century one finds the dreamy man in his desperate quest for the lost Paradise and the practical woman in her fight against the inevitable smites of fate. From birth to death, every individual passes through the four stages of childhood, youth, middle age and old age, too anxiously trying to find out the mystery of existence before one's birth and after one's death. Being motivated by instinctive sex, man searches for the meaning of immortality and seeks many ways to attain it. Of course, through a number of allegorical events and episodes, the philosophy behind the Biblical story of Adam and Eve is made alive; and the word 'Adam' is turned into an equivalent for the Indian theological concept of 'OM', the omnipotent, the omnipresent and the omniscient sound. But my main aim in the novel was to discuss seriously the fate of man, giving much food for thought by adding the spice of an underlying dry humor.

Last but not the least; let me say a few words about this collection of my twenty nine selected short stories titled *Poles Apart on the Same Bed*. The stories are classified into three, representing three stages of my short story writing. Part I consists of ten stories collected from those written during 1981 – 2000; part II consists of eleven stories collected from those written before 1980 and part III consists of eight stories written after the dawn of the third millennium. Though each story is unique in itself, it can be noted that the stories in each part have their own thematic unity. In other words, each story is different in some way or another, although they are the outcome of the same mind and, hence, I believe that the title *Poles Apart on the Same Bed* is not inappropriate. Of course, one of my poems published in *Blossoms, An Anthology of Poems* p.133 (Writers' Forum, Ranchi, India, 2001) has the same title and it is also included in my collection of domestic poems, *Magic Chasm (2007)*. Of course, the collection includes a short story with the same title.

I express my deep gratitude to Dr. S. Subhash Chandran, a critic and an academic, who selected these stories and blessed this work with a preface. I thank the Architecture and Art Historian Jeremy Hespeler-Boultbee, my Canadian colleague at Bahir Dar University, Ethiopia, who read the stories in this collection and showed 'green flag' for its publication. I also thank those publishers in whose periodicals some of the stories in this collection first appeared.

ABOUT THE AUTHOR

Born on April 1st, 1952, Alexander Raju began his career as a freelance journalist as early as 1974, after completing his higher studies in the Universities of Kerala and Saugar, Madhya Pradesh. Touring almost every nook and corner of India, he acquired a firsthand knowledge of the Indian ways of life among various ethnic groups who differed totally in their culture, religion and language. When Sikkim became the twenty-second State of India, he joined the staff of *Sikkim Express* as one of its sub-editors and later became the editor of *Bullet*, a newsweekly published from Gangtok. "A decade of my wanderings through the length and breadth of India and my not too brief sojourn in the Himalayan Valley gave me an everlasting mine of ideas and a continuous source of inspiration that would last a whole lifespan of a creative writer," says the author.

Returning to his native state of Kerala, he worked as a lawyer for a short while. In 1981, he joined the Faculty of English at Baselius College, Kottayam, Kerala, his own alma mater, as a lecturer. During 1996 to 1999, he worked as an Inspector of English, giving training to English teachers, under the Ministry of Education, Sultanate of Oman. For three years, from 2006 to 2009, he served as Associate Professor of English in Bahir Dar University, Ethiopia. Currently he is Professor of English in Al Fateh University, Tripoli, Libya.

Alexander Raju, an Indian English critic, poet, novelist, short story writer and columnist, has many books to his credit. *Ripples and Pebbles* (1989), *Sprouts of Indignation* (2003) and *Magic Chasm* (2007) are collections of his poems. His first novel *The Haunted Man* came out in 1996 and its second edition in 2009. *Upon This Bank and Shoal*, a philosophical novel, came out in 2008. *The Psycho-Social Interface in British Fiction* (2000) is a critical work. *The Voice of Ethiopia and Other Pieces of Literature*, an edited work came out in 2008.

E-mail Alexander Raju: **dr.alexanderraju@yahoo.co.in**

www.ingramcontent.com/pod-product-compliance
Lightning Source LLC
Chambersburg PA
CBHW020837260626
47169CB00003B/1023